The Rovan Binary
(Book 12 of the PIT series)
by Michael McCloskey

ISBN: 978-1729178171

Learn more about Michael McCloskey's works at
www.squidlord.com

Cover art by Stephan Martiniere

Chapter 1

The gray-blue column stood before Telisa like an enigmatic god awaiting supplicants. The room around it was quiet and filled with Terran chairs and Celaran roosting cords. She stepped closer to the artifact that had been moved from a PIT ship into Blackhab.

Her head swam with questions.

How many of these columns exist in our galaxy? How many did the Trilisks make? When was the last one made?

Telisa dispelled the questions from her mind. She knelt before the column, close enough to reach out and touch it. Then she concentrated.

Please... let me have my friends back. We need new copies of them now.

Telisa did not expect to succeed where the Celaran scientists had failed, but she had to try. The column before her was the one that her current Maxsym and Arakaki had with them on a Vovokan *Iridar*. She hoped her host body would lend more authority to her requests. If the column thought she was a Trilisk, it might obey.

She decided to try another tack.

My team is too small. I need specialists to fill it out. Some veteran explorers.

A faint sound came to her ears, magnified threefold by her heightened senses. Someone was behind her! Telisa's host body went into a state of hyper-alertness. Time went into slow motion. Telisa turned and rose to the balls of her feet in one smooth flourish.

An oriental dragon sprawled before her. Its scintillating, green-scaled body rose no taller than she had knelt, though its sinuous body was easily three meters

1

long. Two gorgeous, gold-irised eyes regarded her from an ornate horned skull.

Her face must have fallen. For a moment, she had thought her prayers had worked.

Five save me!

"Hello," it breathed in a half-hiss.

She looked the creature up and down. It did not move to attack her. She sucked in a long breath and let herself relax.

"Are you real?" she asked, forcing her voice to remain level.

"I'm not a hallucination, if that's what you mean," the creature said, managing to look a little put off. "Though I am synthetic, so if you mean am I a real dragon, I suppose the answer might be no."

Did I create this?

"Are you a veteran explorer?" Telisa blurted.

"No. I'm a scientist and a researcher. That's an odd question! I like odd questions."

"I'm Telisa."

"I'm Taishi."

"Is that... with an 'a' and an 'i'?"

"It is, and I am."

An AI.

Telisa had heard of the occasional rich Core Worlder having their brains moved into designer bodies of various types. She supposed it would be even more natural for an AI to live in an exotic artificial body. After all, Adair and Achaius had lived inside Vovokan battle spheres.

"I'm sorry I interrupted. Were you trying to make something?" Taishi asked.

"You *know*?"

"I hoped. I didn't expect it to be true. Is that the Trilisk AI? It looks like any other Trilisk column."

"The existence of the Trilisk AI isn't common knowledge," Telisa said. She did not correct the supposition that the column was a Trilisk AI.

"True. I know more than most. I also know you're the leader of the PIT exploration team."

A PIT exploration team, not THE team. That's two things you don't know.

"What do you research, Taishi?"

"The Trilisks. I believe you and I have that in common."

Telisa cast a glance around the room. For the moment, they appeared to be alone.

"Do you think the Trilisks were evil?" Telisa asked. Before Taishi could answer, she continued. "I mean, do you think they were cruel, selfish, power-hungry? Did any of them have respect for other, less-advanced life forms?"

"I don't know," Taishi said. "I think there is evidence that indicates some of them were cruel. It's open to interpretation. I don't know how many of them existed and how much variation there was among them. Do you have the answers? Will you share your knowledge with me?"

"I've been given brief glimpses into their memories, even experienced life as a Trilisk for a short time. Everything I've learned has disappointed me," she said. "Only their staggering technological achievements have lived up to my childhood imagination of them."

"So… what are you trying to make?" Taishi asked.

"I'm trying to get the column to release new copies of my dead crew members."

The dragon smiled the long, toothy smile of a reptilian Cheshire.

"Ahhhhh. That would be another odd thing to say, if you weren't who you are, and if you weren't standing in front of an ancient Trilisk artifact."

"Do you work for the Space Force?"

The creature regarded her for a long second. Its scaly tail flopped to one side. She heard the long rasp of an inhalation.

"I have in the past. I've since earned my freedom, though I still do what I've always done for them... though now, for myself."

"Good," Telisa said. "I hope you can master these mysteries someday," she said sincerely.

"Please tell me of your crew. Why do you think the column can emit new copies of people?"

"I know it can. I've been copied, myself. This column knows my friends. It can recreate them."

"But it won't? It has a choice?"

"It's not clear to me. Shiny is the only one I know of who has ever used it on demand."

"Ahhhhh. Ambassador Shiny. That one holds its cards close to the thorax."

Telisa had nothing to say about that. Taishi was certainly correct.

"We seem to be alone. Does that mean it's not working?" Taishi asked.

"It's not working," Telisa verified. "Unless you were on the PIT team at some point?"

"Not that I recall. Wouldn't you be able to remember?"

Telisa shook her head slowly.

"Not necessarily. It's complicated."

Taishi seemed pleased by her statements. Perhaps he found her mysterious; or perhaps he understood that working with Trilisk artifacts might cause highly unusual things to happen. Unusual, at least, for a Terran.

"I will try to accomplish this feat, both for you, and for myself," Taishi hissed. "Tell me: if I can get your team out, would you be grateful?"

"Yes," Telisa said quickly. "Of course."

"Grateful enough to let me study the Trilisk AI up close? To teach me to use it?"

Telisa looked at Taishi in all its grandeur. Did she dare trust this intelligent stranger?

Using the AI is a lot easier than you know.

She pointed at her backpack sitting by the edge of the platform.

"Tell me what you want, Taishi. Keep it small, please."

"I already—"

"Ask me for something small first," Telisa insisted.

"I would like... a gold coin with my image on it," Taishi said.

Telisa walked over to her pack. She knelt down and unzipped one of the smallest pockets. She fished through it with her fingers until she felt the heavy coin and brought it out. She turned and presented it to Taishi.

"I agree to your terms. Consider this your down payment," Telisa said.

For a dragon, Taishi looked suitably impressed.

Michael McCloskey

Chapter 2

"Lee! Thank you for meeting me," Telisa said. She stood next to Lee in a vine grove on the inside surface of Blackhab. The vines had grown as thick as Telisa's legs in places. The largest leaves were only a quarter of a meter in diameter so far, but their shape and color reminded Telisa of the huge vines she had discovered on Celaran worlds.

Above them, Celaran houses floated in midair as far as the Terran eye could see.

"Of course! I'm so glad to see the team resting on our vine again!" Lee replied electronically.

"Where is your team going?" Telisa asked.

Lee performed an aerial loop, then flew around Telisa in a tight circle.

"We'll be flying far to another Rovan vine," Lee said. "I'm excited to go! We have Celarans like myself and also cyborgs to protect us."

"That's good. I'm excited for you. I know you'll be very cautious, too. I don't want any harm to come to you or your team."

"Of course we will be! What did you want to chat about over the sap?"

"I wanted to discuss an issue with the new teams. When we recruited our new scientists... we neglected a problem. If they live and study at Blackhab, then they'll be within range of the Trilisk AI."

"Oh. I think that will be fine, since we're all working together to share the secrets of aliens across the galactic arm!"

"Well, I had hoped to keep the AI a secret of our own. Though I admit, a few in the Space Force know... maybe

7

I'm dumb to even hope that Shiny doesn't know. But most Terrans aren't aware of such powerful Trilisk artifacts."

"It helps everyone on the vine. Why keep secrets?" Lee asked innocently.

Telisa sighed. She felt like a subverter and a protector at the same time.

"To avoid having someone come to take it by force. I also want to remind you and Cynan that you have to keep preparing for such a dark day. I know you abhor war, but you must remain vigilant. Between the many threats you face, the Celarans must keep honing your new military."

They don't even have that word. I think in their language they say 'dangerous tool experts'.

"We are. We try. I'm sorry, but I don't know how to solve the problem with the AI."

"I just wanted your view on it. Sounds like you would let them know. Thank you."

"Good luck!"

"And to you," Telisa said. Lee shot off into the sky. Telisa followed the alien's serpentine form until it receded into a dot in the distance.

Telisa needed to travel to her own meeting with the new Terran arrivals she had mentioned: young scientists dedicated to the assimilation of alien technical knowledge. It was the first step toward Telisa's latest goal of disseminating PIT's know-how to Terrans in general.

She had been looking forward to traveling through Blackhab the old-fashioned way as pioneered by Caden and Siobhan.

Telisa crouched, readying the power in her legs, then sprang upward with tremendous force. She broke away from the light gravity zone the station provided on its inner surface and flew 'upward' toward the floating houses of the interior. Her three attendant spheres shot after her.

She allowed herself to relax and soar through the air. The warm light of the simulated sky felt wonderful on the skin of her face. For a while, Telisa just enjoyed being alive.

Her attendants nudged her course so she could launch off from another house a few hundred meters distant. She landed, then jumped toward the next. Thus she traveled for several kilometers until she came to the building where her FTF was scheduled.

She hit the roof and walked over to the nearest circular hatch with a mind to open it and drop down to the room below. Her sharp eyes caught sight of a group of people who had spotted her from inside.

They must have heard the thump when I landed.

She could make an even more exciting entrance. She allowed herself to think about it.

It might inspire them even further if I vault in there Trilisk Special Forces style... but that's an excuse right? An excuse to show off and bask in their amazement. No. I should downplay it and focus on them and the adventure they're about to undertake.

Telisa walked on by the hatch and continued on until she was out of sight of those inside. She chose a different hatch and entered the building out of their sight.

Once inside, she oriented herself using her link and walked into the meeting room like a normal Terran.

Telisa took a couple of seconds to size up the room. Four young Terran adults sat around a table that had been installed in the building along with many other Terran amenities. They each stared at her and her orbiting attendants with a sense of awe. One rose to a ramrod-straight standing position, then the other three followed.

They're nervous to meet a TM.

"Please relax. Thank you for coming. I'm glad to see there are people who want to learn about the alien technologies so much that they'll come all the way out here to work with the Celarans."

Two of the scientists relaxed noticeably. The other two shifted slightly as if in response, but failed to relax at all. Telisa took a seat. The scientists sat back down.

"Please introduce yourselves. Let's get to know each other a little bit." Telisa nodded toward a young man on her right. The scientist had short black hair and olive skin.

"I'm Randal," he said. "I used to head up the Space Force's Celaran tech integration team. As you know, since we formed the Celaran Pact, we've been working on infrastructure that helps the interchange of mathematics, device designs, and modular components between Terrans and Celarans. Now, I'm very happy to come here and further my studies of Celaran technology. I'm a biology specialist, so I'll be focusing on that area."

To his credit, the young scientist sounded more enthusiastic than nervous. Telisa smiled and looked at the next person, who had a light brown complexion and a spiral hair pattern that lazily shifted according to a Core World style. She was exceptionally beautiful.

"My name is Celeste. Let me say first, on behalf of all of us, thank you and the rest of the PIT team for releasing this huge body of information to us for study. We owe you so much," she said. For a split second all the spirals in her hair lined up like a stack of cylinders, then it returned to spiral chaos again.

Telisa nodded. She felt a little guilty.

We collected most of that for our own personal gain. But at least, we're sharing it now.

Celeste continued.

"I was a liaison in the Space Force working on integrating the Vovokan weapons Shiny gave us to fight the Destroyers, or now, the Quarus as we call them. So I'm here to keep learning about Vovokan technology."

A weapons expert. That's good, but we need more Vovokan computer specialists like Cilreth and Marcant.

The next scientist looked older than the rest and did not advertise a gender. The person had light skin and hair with a freckled face.

"I'm Diana. I've studied the original Quarus spacecraft extensively. Needless to say, my career has gone from a dead end to a supernova given recent events. So I've come here to learn more with the Celarans... and the PIT team."

"Were the real Quarus anything like you had imagined?" Telisa asked, trying to coax more from Diana.

"No... not at all like I imagined, TM."

Telisa considered telling them all to call her Telisa, then she decided not to. If she was going to settle into a real leadership position, perhaps she should stop telling everyone that.

The last scientist looked less like an academic than the others, though Telisa could not put her finger on just why. He had thick brown hair, light skin, and a strong aquiline nose.

"Hello, everyone. I'm Trevor, assigned to assimilation of Rovan technology."

Eyebrows went up around the table.

"...Rovan?" Randal asked uncertainly.

11

"Our newest find," Telisa said. "We brought a significant batch of tech in from a new ruins site. Very promising technology."

Trevor leaned forward and spoke rapidly.

"Yes. It's a lot to take in, but I've been working through it every spare moment. The PIT team has amassed a huge amount of information about them. In particular, their mastery of force fields is striking."

Ah, to be young again.

"I'm very happy to see bright young minds tackling these projects," Telisa said to those assembled around her. "This work is so very important. Working together, we will..."

To sugarcoat or not to sugarcoat?

"...increase the chances that Terrans survive in a hostile universe," Telisa finished.

The scientists looked suitably impressed by the gravitas of their mission.

"I want to stress one aspect of your official missions," Telisa said. "We all want to learn all about these technologies, and I know that can be the most fascinating part. But we need to continue to *integrate* them into our technology. Even with our advances in modularizing many components, we can't go on forever with ships made from Vovokan this, Celaran that, and Rovan the-other-thing. We need to integrate these into Terran *everything*, so that we truly know how to make it and how to use it. And we need to get better at continually integrating new things that come along. I'm glad to hear some of you have already been involved in that process. Integration is always a gritter engineering problem, uglier than the pure pursuit of knowledge, but it's what we need."

12

Telisa stopped for a beat.

"Any questions?"

Diana squirmed in her seat. Telisa looked at her and smiled a little, trying to encourage her.

"Why isn't there a Trilisk specialist?" Diana asked.

"I'm one of the Trilisk specialists," Telisa said. "And the Celarans have many more." She thought of Taishi, but decided not to mention it. "But that's not the real answer. To be perfectly honest, I've started to wonder if perhaps the old Space Force was justified in their policies of keeping certain technologies from the public. We've seen Trilisk artifacts that can destroy entire planets, and I don't even think they qualified as weapons in the eyes of their makers."

The conversation paused. Eventually Celeste asked another question.

"A large percentage of the information I have on Vovokan technology was curated by Magnus," Celeste said. "Er, TM Garrison. Will I have the chance to meet him?"

The young scientist utterly failed to mask her admiration and hope.

Oh dear.

"You will meet him eventually," Telisa stumbled. "Probably not before our next mission, though."

"You're leaving?" Trevor asked.

"Yes. I won't be around to watch over your shoulder. You've all proven your professionalism or you wouldn't be here. We'll come back with even more for you to study, Trevor."

Celeste took another turn.

"Do these positions come with any possibility of joining the PIT team someday?" she asked.

Telisa stared at the wisp of a scientist, looking first at her slender arms, delicate skin, and subtle Core Worlder facial decorations.

"Only if you're unlucky," Telisa said.

Chapter 3

Magnus sat lotus-style in his quarters and puzzled over the Celaran-sourced star charts in his PV. The room was quiet and dark. A laser pistol and a long combat knife lay within easy reach.

The foremost pane in his mind was an interface to the Celaran star repository on Blackhab. The closest system that Marcant had decoded as a Rovan colony site was a binary system. The information the Celarans had collected on the system indicated it was a paired main-sequence star and neutron star. The system would likely be awash in deadly radiation and gravitational instability.

Why would Rovans make a colony there?

Magnus opened a link channel to Marcant and Telisa.

"Marcant. Have you looked at the closest Rovan colony site in the Celaran star repository?"

"No. What's up?"

"I'm not sure this intel is good," Magnus said. "There's a couple of planets there... but in a binary system with a neutron star. Doesn't sound like a great place to live."

"That *is* odd. Maybe we misinterpreted what the system locations meant," Marcant said. "Obviously there was a Rovan colony in the Rovatick system, and it was part of this map. There were other contextual clues, such as repeated blocks of information we decided were descriptions of the storage sites. We thought the similar blocks associated with these other locations were the same things."

"I might see Vovokans going there, since they live way underground. But Rovans?" Magnus protested. "Does the data say *why*?"

"We're not to the point where we understand all the data. Note, though, one of these bodies is a fairly big rocky planet," Marcant said. "Perhaps it managed to hold on to some of its atmosphere even with the neutron star around."

"And we have a few reasons to believe Rovans might be comfortable in higher gravity than we are," Telisa said.

"Still... I'm doubtful," Magnus said.

"All the more reason to go there," Telisa said. "You have me curious. I agree that this sounds like a suboptimal place to set up a colony. So let's go see why they did so."

"Sure," Magnus said.

"My records show you haven't visited the column yet," Telisa said to Magnus.

"So now I'm being spied upon?" Magnus asked mildly, even though he did not mind Telisa's concern.

"Don't make me pull rank on you, TM," Telisa replied.

"Yes, ma'am. I'm headed over there now," Magnus said.

"Can you meet up with Maxsym? He's supposed to go over there, too. He's the only other one besides you that hasn't yet."

"Will do."

Magnus found Maxsym on the *Sharplight*'s map. He was headed for the shuttles already.

"Meet you there?" Magnus asked over his link.

"Certainly," Maxsym replied.

As Magnus walked through the massive warship, he recalled his time in the war against the UED. The

16

Sharplight would have been a welcome ally to him then. He had never been anywhere near a capital ship during his time in the Space Force.

Life is strange. I'm not even in the Force anymore, but I could command a ship like this as a TM. At least, as long as Shiny willed it so.

When Magnus arrived at the bay, Maxsym met him next to a Vovokan shuttle. They let themselves inside and told the shuttle to bring them to Blackhab.

"So what have you been working on, Maxsym?"

"Telisa's genome," Maxsym said.

Magnus was surprised.

"The Trilisk host bodies?" Magnus prompted.

"Yes. We're trying to unravel the secret to the remote control problem. It's slow going. I wouldn't get any hopes up."

Magnus knew that if Maxsym said it was slow going, he meant it. Maxsym tended to plow through major problems as quickly as Marcant; Maxsym's current description meant this was a problem that might not be solvable at all.

"Yourself?" asked Maxsym.

"The usual. We need robots that can fight rovlings."

"Yes. That sounds good, just in case."

The shuttle ride was quick. Soon they reached Blackhab's outer surface and slipped into a pressurized zone. The two strode out of the shuttle into an airy bay. On the PIT team's first visit to Blackhab, he had thought the bays were so huge because of the potential shapes of vessels that might come to rest there, but now he knew that the Celarans had made it that way so there was plenty of room to fly around above the vessels.

17

A few Celarans flitted about. It looked like they were playing, but that did not mean much. To Magnus, the Celarans looked like they were playing even when they worked. He saw one holding a second tool rod and supposed that was as good an indication as any that the Celaran intended to get something repaired or built.

The Trilisk pillar was not far from the access point they had chosen. Magnus followed a map provided by his link. Maxsym walked along beside him.

"I never thought I would be coming to a place like this to pray," Maxsym said.

"I know what you mean," Magnus replied. They took a right and walked down an access corridor. A Celaran flitted by, headed in the opposite direction. Up ahead, a large room held the Trilisk pillar in its center.

They entered and slowed. Magnus was uncertain if he had to be very close to the pillar or if anywhere nearby could work. He supposed no one knew.

"Magnus?"

Magnus turned to view the speaker. A slender young woman with light brown skin and intricate hair had addressed him. Her eyes were striking and delicately decorated.

"Yes, I'm Magnus," he said.

"I'm Celeste. I'm very glad I got the chance to meet you before you left on your mission," Celeste said. She put out her hand with knuckles facing him and fingers dipped low.

Magnus mirrored her presentation with his hand, then let his knuckles slightly touch hers. The ritual was a Core Worlder gesture of greeting that had originally been a modified handshake without any incarnate touching. A decade after that, touching the knuckles anyway had developed as an expression of warm acceptance. While Core Worlders carried on with great abandon in their shared virtual worlds, incarnate touching was considered very intimate and special. Frontier writers had concluded that Core Worlders were "demons incorporeal, angels incarnate".

Celeste smiled grandly.

"I wanted to thank you personally for all the information you've compiled on Vovokan technology," Celeste said. "The robotics section, in particular, was *so* detailed."

She looks Core World, not frontier...

"Oh. I'm glad you find it helpful. Are you one of the scientists we invited here to learn with the Celarans?"

"Yes. I'm from Drasma," she said dismissively. "You're in your armor! I heard you wear it everywhere. Always ready for action." Her eyes openly examined his form. Then she reached out and actually touched the shoulder of his Veer suit.

"I feel uncomfortable without it," Magnus said. "It's common enough out this far."

The young woman stared at him intensely as if memorizing every word. He glanced over at Maxsym, who had taken several steps past them and dropped to his knees facing the pillar.

She followed his eyes.

"Is he... *praying* to that pillar?" Celeste whispered.

"I believe he's just concentrating," Magnus deflected. "We have some routine data updates to perform. Nothing very interesting, I'm afraid."

"You exchange data with the Trilisk artifact!" Celeste breathed in awe.

Magnus shrugged. "Believe me, that doesn't mean we've conquered the secrets of the Trilisks." He turned slightly away from her and faced Maxsym, preparing to move over toward the pillar. She understood his body language.

"Well I hate to keep you... if you have to leave soon?"

"Sorry, I do. I wish you the best of luck though, Celeste. It's an important mission you have."

Celeste took a small step closer.

"How long will you be gone? May I get in touch with you when you return? I might have questions about the Vovokan data."

Magnus got the impression that 'might' was not the right word. He felt it was more of a 'definitely'.

"I'm hardly the expert you seem to think I am," Magnus said. "I'm just a soldier. You probably already know a good deal more about Vovokan technology than I do."

Celeste's mouth froze in an 'O' of surprise. Then she began a rapid-fire plea.

"Please, TM, don't dismiss your skills so readily! You made incredible insights in your summary and backed them up in amazing detail... I think we could both benefit from working closely together. I know you must have many pressing for your attention, but I promise I won't waste your time."

She leaned forward, almost touching him. Magnus generally did not like fragile women, but something about her delicate physique grabbed his attention despite himself. He hesitated, trying to figure out why he wanted to respond positively.

Has it simply been too long since I was the physically strong one in a relationship? Is there some male instinct for that?

Maxsym came to the rescue.

"I've finished. It either has me or it doesn't," he said.

"Ah. I need to hurry then. Maxsym, this is Celeste," Magnus said, then walked away toward the pillar. He stopped about two meters from the smooth gray surface and closed his eyes.

Back me up. Remember me. Keep me on file. I might die. Remember me so you can make another one of me, please. Thank you.

When he finished, he stood and listened facing the pillar. He still heard Celeste's voice, presumably in conversation with Maxsym. Was she as interested in each TM? Magnus hoped so. It would be easier to deal with a general PIT fan than someone who had a thing for him personally.

"Why does he always wear that huge knife on his thigh?" Celeste was asking.

"An armed society is a polite society," Maxsym said.

"What? Where's that from?" she asked.

"Forgive me, it's ancient. I'm a student of history."

"I don't know why you would care about ancient times. People like Magnus are making important history right now!"

Damn.

Magnus turned and walked back. Celeste still stood next to Maxsym. She smiled again as Magnus approached.

"It was nice to meet you Celeste. We have to head back now," Magnus asserted.

"I'm so happy we could chat," Celeste said. She stared right into Magnus's eyes. Magnus nodded curtly and walked off with Maxsym in tow.

"She seems very interested in TMs," he remarked over a private channel to Maxsym.

"I don't know. She just asked a bunch of questions about you," Maxsym said flatly.

Damn.

Chapter 4

Adair hovered in the corner and watched Magnus.

The ex-UNSF soldier stood with his eyes closed before a shiny new robot with six legs. The body looked like little more than a flexible chassis to connect the six legs, three on each side. Six attendants had been harnessed at the trunk near each leg connection. A flat power supply housing an energy storage ring sat nestled in the center. Each end of the robot had an identical sensor cluster, so it had no set head or tail.

Magnus opened his eyes.

"Okay, try out your new body," Magnus said.

The body combined several features Adair had requested. It had a high manipulation capability, as each of the six limbs could serve as either a leg or a hand: each ended in four opposing fingers that folded together to form a pointed "foot" when the limb was used for walking.

The chassis was light, so much so that the six attendants could lift it into the air, though only for a short time. When paired with the attendants, the body could leap ten meters into the air in one g.

Adair floated down and attached itself to the center of the chassis.

"For combat applications, the body is built to accept one of our new force field packs, but the weight of the pack negates the amazing agility," Magnus said. "Sorry, but you'll have to choose between durability and maneuverability."

"I understand, Magnus. Tradeoffs must be made."

Adair walked around the bay on all six legs. After one quick circle, it brought up its two front limbs as arms and walked around on the back four. It stopped to pick up one of Magnus's tools. The body worked flawlessly.

"Thank you, Magnus. This should be very useful. It feels... very nice to have a unique body all my own."

"Take a tour. Visit everyone in your new digs," Magnus suggested. "I'll expect you to come back later with a list of bugs, or ideas for enhancement. Don't hesitate to ask for changes. It will help you improve your body and it will help me learn."

"I will!" Adair said.

Adair made a request to *Sharplight* to provide a visitor route for the remaining crew. The ship showed Telisa's location nearby. She was first. Adair scampered off on the agile legs.

Adair viewed the first corridor through its new body's sensors. It could see from the sensor clusters on each end of the chassis, as well those on its current attendant container. The corridor was empty. It ran down the corridor and took a left before coming to an open doorway. *Sharplight* indicated that Telisa was inside.

Telisa greeted Adair with laser drawn. Adair stopped.

"It's me, Adair. I'm sorry if I startled you."

Telisa paused. Adair verified that she was in link contact with Magnus.

She put her weapon away.

"Your body is unfamiliar."

"Hey, Adair," Magnus said at the same time on a private channel. "I put you on the default friendlies list served from the armory. That should keep you from getting shot until everyone gets used to you. Sorry about the oversight."

"That's fine, Magnus. Thank you."

Adair addressed Telisa aloud, using its body's hardware.

"How did you react so quickly? I turned the corner to a drawn gun."

"I didn't recognize the sound of your footsteps," she said. "You walk differently than Magnus's other robots. Hey, are those fingers at the ends of your legs?"

"Yes! Each of these six legs ends in a hand," Adair said, lifting a leg. The fingers sprung outward, displaying the range of motion of each with its three joints. The fingers currently sat ninety degrees apart from each other, but they could rotate independently around the leg, enabling Adair to form a Terran-like hand by sliding three fingers together and leaving the fourth opposed like a thumb. It would be useful for grasping tools specialized for Terran use, like pistols.

"What are you doing today?" Adair asked.

"Building OCP training scenarios. I've got some Quarus and Rovan combat runs, free-form exploration, and unknown alien encounters," she said.

"To which OCP do you refer?"

"Orbs, Claws, and Packs. You know, Celaran stealth orbs, breaker claws, and the Rovan force field packs. It's our new combo that every PIT member will have in the field."

"Ah. You could add a V for the Veer suits," Adair said.

"We could! But there's too many pieces of Terran standard equipment to feed into the acronym. Veer suits, PAWs, lasers, swords, grenades... it goes on and on."

"Do you want S or SB for stun baton? We could standardize on VOCPAWLGS since that rolls off the Terran tongue nicely."

"Uhm, no. The Terran equipment is assumed. It's our alien standard issues that I'm focusing on."

"Okay," Adair said.

"If you want to help, I'd appreciate it if you could build a single difficulty input into the scenarios so that we can better auto-adjust the difficulty on the fly based on our performance," Telisa said. "We already have basic difficulty knobs, but the trick is, I want to adjust the parameters in unpredictable ways. I don't want the team to anticipate what's next by knowing that the difficulty is going up or down."

"So, for instance, if the difficulty increases by one step, they can't expect to simply fight one more enemy; instead it might be that they fight *fewer* enemies but experience equipment malfunctions and disadvantageous terrain?"

"Exactly."

"Sure, I can do that. Send me a pointer when you're done with the setups."

"Thanks. Hey, did I already thank you for the solution you implemented for letting us breathe in the force fields?"

"You did, but it wasn't really me. The Rovans made their packs to allow oxygen through the screen, and I simply copied their work."

"Just another piece of evidence that the packs were for the Rovans. They breathed something like us," Telisa said.

"Yes, I think so."

"What happens in water?" Telisa asked.

"It draws more power but you stay dry," Adair said.

Telisa shook her head. "Amazing."

"Well, see you later," Adair said.

Telisa smiled and nodded, then she went off-retina.

The *Sharplight* told Adair that Yat and Arakaki were in Arakaki's quarters. Adair left Telisa's room and strode down the corridor to visit them.

Let's try some acrobatics!

As an experiment, Adair performed a few quick calculations and prepared the results as "reflexes" for its body. Then it leaped up, putting more thrust on the right side. The body spun in mid-air, allowing all six legs to contact the ceiling. As soon as it landed there, Adair introduced more spin force pushing from the ceiling, anticipating that the additional acceleration toward the floor would give less time to finish the spin.

Adair landed on all six legs. The contact with the floor occurred slightly off the expected timing, but Adair's legs were able to absorb the anomaly. Adair made adjustments and saved the maneuver away.

Pretty fun body!

Adair made an agile turn at the end of one corridor and took another. It came to a deck-connector tube and rose to the next deck in a single elegant leap, assisted by the six attendants attached to its chassis.

Outside Arakaki's quarters, Adair paused. It detected a slight vibration, below the threshold of Terran sensory capabilities. After a pause, another thump. There was a rhythm to it.

Yat and Arakaki's links said they were unavailable.

They're most likely having fun, too. I suppose I shouldn't interrupt. It would just make them dislike me and my new body. Terrans are so very dependent upon first impressions!

Adair culled them from the visit list and let *Sharplight* direct the way toward Marcant. As it turned out, Maxsym was with Marcant in an observation lounge. Adair ran though the ship to join them.

"Team, we have an anomaly," Barrai said on the PIT channel. "I see an unknown sig, central corridor, deck five, but somehow it's on the armory no fire list."

"Stand down, it's one of my robots," Magnus said. "Experimental model. I should have told *Sharplight* when I updated the friendlies list. Sorry."

Adair appreciated how Magnus had not revealed that Adair was in the new robot.

Very thoughtful of him not to spoil my surprise!

The lounge had an outer curved wall that usually looked like a window into space, though it was actually a shared augmented reality display sent through their links. Today the curved wall displayed huge diagrams of biological structures.

Marcant spoke to Maxsym as Adair bounced in.

"Here are the parts of the host body neurons that are tuned to receive the remote signals. What I'm hoping you could answer is: can Telisa live without these segments of the host... let's call it DNA since it's beyond anything I understand?"

Maxsym released a string of tight syllables unfamiliar to Adair. A side process solved the question: Maxsym emitted Russian curses. The conversation sounded important, so Adair only eavesdropped.

"What?" Marcant asked. "You've already identified these parts?"

"I've struggled to understand those segments for so long. But I was thinking of them as RNA-analogue transcribers. But they're not doing anything like that..."

"They're sensitive to electromagnetic signals at several frequencies," Marcant said. "But only in the neural cells, as far as I can tell. It was these key differences in the neurons that first attracted me to these structures."

"Yes, and you've told me what they do. I know of no other function for them," Maxsym said.

"Could it really be that easy? Just snip, snip, snip and—"

"It might be," Maxsym breathed.

"But if we're wrong, it would kill her?"

"It could. More likely the danger would be destroying her intellect. We might be able to try applying the changes incrementally. Cautiously. Unlike other parts of the body, we won't be able to just wait for the edited neural cells to split, unless we artificially induce production of new ones, but that's a structural problem."

"Can we simulate—"

"No. Not with host bodies. That works fine for Terran cells, but the Trilisk cells are beyond our abilities to simulate. The best test would be to remove a few cells and test it outside her body."

"Remove brain cells? Who would go for that?"

"I can identify ones that haven't been recruited for important things," Maxsym said dismissively.

Adair did not dare to interrupt with its own humble news. Instead, it joined the conversation.

"You could grow a new brain without these structures and see if it thrived. Then, if that test succeeds, you would have reason to believe you could use nanomachines to edit these structures from Telisa's neurons without harming her."

"Who is that? Adair? It's a fair suggestion, though it takes time and it's not conclusive," Maxsym said. "Besides, what would we do with the new person? Tell them sorry, they're just an experiment?"

"Any better ideas?"

"We could ask Telisa," Marcant said.

"I want something more solid first," Maxsym said. "You know Telisa. She will feel obligated to take a big risk to keep the team safe. I'd rather have a plan worked out with a high chance of success before we bring it up."

"Yeah, you're right," Marcant said.

"You hide this discovery from our leader?" Adair asked.

"Hey, don't let her know yet," Marcant said. "We'll tell her when it's solid, I promise."

"I won't tell her."

"Is that you over there?" Maxsym asked. An attendant flitted over to look at Adair.

"Yes. Magnus made this for me."

"Very nice!" Marcant said. "It's about time he did something to repay you for all that work you did on his combat designs."

"Repayment wasn't necessary," Adair said. "Being able to fight off rovlings benefits all of us."

"Well, it looks good," Maxsym said. "Very versatile, I think?"

"Yes, it is. Thanks."

Adair moved on.

Barrai was on one of *Sharplight*'s bridges. Adair ran there, testing its body again. When it skittered into the room, Barrai turned and leveled a pistol at Adair.

"Again? It's me, Adair."

"Is it really?" Barrai said coldly. "I can override this friendly list in an instant, if I have to," she warned.

"Well... yes, it's really me."

"Why are you on the bridge?"

"To visit you!"

She put the pistol away and seemed to relax a notch.

"What's up? I haven't seen this robot before."

"I'm taking it for a spin."

"It looks light. Must be fast."

"It is! What are you doing?" Adair asked, daring to take a few steps forward.

"Analyzing the Rovan beam used to neutralize our intruder. I want to be able to reproduce it perfectly, in case we run into another... entity... like that again."

"I've been working on containment protocols for that. But it seems like finding the brain and shutting it down is the most important."

"Seems like it. Why this beam, do you think?" Barrai asked. She shared some data with Adair. "It doesn't even interact very much with solid matter."

"It would decohere entangled particles," Adair said. "Must be a weakness of whatever that creature was."

"You would call it a creature?"

"For lack of a better term," Adair conceded.

"Well, I hope it's one of a kind," Barrai said.

"I doubt it was," Adair said.

"You're supposed to just agree," Barrai said. "You know, share the sentiment and not stir up the ugly facts."

"Oh. Sorry. Well, if we find one in another of those force field cages, we'll leave it alone. So maybe we won't have to fight one again."

"Better," Barrai said.

Chapter 5

Magnus was awake when the *Sharplight* arrived at their destination, so he stopped in to one of the armored bridges to watch the action with Telisa. Fresh out of a workout, Magnus felt sore. The blue lounge chair he spotted beckoned to him. He settled into it with a sigh of relief. Telisa, ever active and invulnerable, did not sit; instead, she paced the room end to end. Barrai sat across from them while the rest of the PIT team remained remote.

"Probes away," Barrai said over the team channel.

The probes shot toward the ordinary star in the binary system auto-designated as Guiholda Conchallon. More information poured in about two rocky planets near the star. The first was too close and too hot for any life remotely like Terrans. The second was cooler, but despite being twenty percent more massive than Earth, it had not retained any significant atmosphere.

The conditions in this system are inimical to Terrans, Magnus thought. *Could Rovans really live here?*

"Our target planet is a dry rock. No appreciable atmosphere. It's also getting a generous helping of gamma rays," Barrai reported.

"The neutron star may have stripped everything away," Adair said on the team channel. "It's definitely causing a lot of the gamma radiation. Material from this system is being sucked into the neutron star, and some of it is superheated on the way in."

"Is the *Sharplight* in danger?"

"Not at these levels. This isn't much radiation on a cosmic scale."

33

"It's only a trickle compared to a pulsar, but it's enough to kill on that planet," Marcant said.

"We should check it out up close," Telisa said. "There might be ruins under the surface. Or even a Trilisk base."

"Wouldn't the Trilisks be bored here? They like to play with other life forms, it seems," Arakaki said bitterly.

"This planet may once have held life. The Trilisks might have been here," Telisa said, though she did not sound like she thought it likely.

Four probes descended on the planet while the *Sharplight* approached. More data flowed in, but nothing looked encouraging.

"We've struck out," Marcant said.

"Happens to the best of us, jelly-brain," Adair replied.

Telisa did not reach the conclusion as quickly.

"How about water? Anything?" she asked.

"Several subsurface lakes found," Barrai reported. Transparent blue blobs appeared on the shared map.

"Mostly near the ice caps, except that one," Telisa said. "Concentrate your scans there."

"Aye," Barrai replied.

The underground lake she had referenced looked more like a wide river; it had an irregular shape almost twenty kilometers long that never grew to a kilometer in width.

"What's holding up the cavern?" Magnus asked.

"A shelf of iron and nickel," Barrai said. "It must be extraplanetary in origin."

That perked Telisa up. "Is it—"

"It has a natural structure. A very old meteorite is the most likely explanation," Barrai said. "It is highly unusual, but not a sign of alien design, I'd say. More of a statistical anomaly."

Telisa deflated.

"What's that?" Adair asked. It pinged a spot on the edge of the underground body of water.

"I... don't know," Barrai said. She recruited another ship sensor to zero in on the spot. Magnus magnified his map. A complex column of carbon and metal appeared.

"Okay, now *that's* designed," Barrai said.

"Yes!" Telisa exulted.

"How did you know?" Marcant asked. Magnus assumed he was asking Telisa.

"It's an interesting spot," Telisa said. "If you wanted to stay here, it's a compelling choice, assuming you're a life form that needs water for sustenance or industry."

"I suppose, but wouldn't you have to worry about caving in the lake?" Yat asked.

"We'll see," Telisa said. "Send ten attendants ahead. Magnus and I are going in."

"Need any more?" Arakaki asked eagerly.

"Arakaki and Yat in the backup shuttle," Telisa said. "If it's a Rovan site, we'll send for you. The rest of you keep looking for other sites."

Magnus shared Telisa's excitement as they hurried out of the bridge. They picked up a fresh anti-rovling weapons suite in an armory near the lab where they had been produced. Telisa beat Magnus out of the room. He strode out toward his quarters to get his favorite gear.

Less than ten minutes later, Magnus met back up with their leader at one of the *Sharplight*'s shuttle bays.

"Don't forget your oxygen membranes," Maxsym said on the team channel. "Though there's no guarantee that the water in that lake would be oxygenated."

I was hoping we'd never need those again.

"I bet there's air in there," Telisa said. "But point taken. We're going into an alien tower adjacent to a huge subterranean lake."

"I've got it," Magnus told her.

Magnus did a quick check to see where they had stored the Quarus incursion gear. He told a couple of his robots to run off and fetch the membranes. By the time the machines returned, Arakaki and Yat had showed up to prep their shuttle. Telisa and Magnus draped the membranes across their backs and connected the umbilicals to their Veer suits. Then they each slipped on a flat Rovan pack over that, and finally backpacks filled with gear.

Telisa disappeared up the ramp. Magnus gave Arakaki and Yat a wave and followed. They sealed up the craft and left for the mysterious find on the rocky planet below.

Telisa turned toward him in the shuttle.

"Attendant feeds are coming in. First two on the scene verify it's Rovan," Telisa told him.

"So the coordinates mean something after all," Magnus said.

"This is important," Telisa said. "Such an unusual location, and hidden."

"It might have been hidden, or it might be that sitting next to that old meteorite shelf, it's hard to detect."

"You're on," Telisa sent to Arakaki and Yat.

"Let's hope there's a front door," Telisa said to Magnus.

The rocky planet grew in the feeds as they descended. The first thing Magnus noted was the utter lack of clouds or other atmospheric effects. The surface resolved into a rough brown wasteland. The shuttle joined the lead attendants hovering over the site.

"I don't see it," Magnus said. The surface did not seem to have any clues as to the structure below. Magnus thought he saw a subtle change in the surface looking out over the lake, but he could not be sure. The meteorite must have fallen a very long time ago.

"Over here," Telisa said, guiding the shuttle down with her link.

Magnus kept looking. Finally he saw a light gray hexagon set into the rocks. The structure was about ten meters wide. The attendant's scan showed a composition of carbon, alloys of titanium, aluminum... and lead. Structural members crisscrossed the surface, connecting the vertices of the hexagonal shape.

"Radiation shielding, looks like," Telisa summarized. "I'll land over here. The rocks are uneven, but should be doable. I don't want to damage the shielding."

The shuttle dropped, then clanked and listed. Magnus tensed and waited until it settled. He checked the tactical. It showed that at least they were not resting above the lake.

"As good as we're going to get," Telisa said. "Let's hit it!"

Magnus deployed his suit's faceplate and exited his seat with a grunt of effort. Telisa opened the rear hatch and leaped out confidently. Magnus followed more cautiously. The extra pull of the planet was onerous. Carrying the full OCP plus the membrane was compounding the problem.

I'm sure Trilisk Special Forces can handle it.

The attendants had not found any dangers other than the rocks and the lack of atmosphere. The planet had some volcanic activity, but none near the unusual lake they had found.

Arakaki set the other shuttle down a hundred meters away on the far side of the Rovan facility. Telisa was already walking the perimeter of the hexagonal surface.

Magnus stepped across the rocks. His legs complained.

Okay, bad timing for my workout. Now I'm going to be wiped out.

He moved sluggishly. Magnus stomped over to the edge of the hexagon. The triangles formed by the support beams were set slightly deeper than the beams. He scanned for doors, sensor bulges, or anything that might give a clue as to what the place was or how to enter it.

"If it doesn't have a door, then we may have to cut in," Telisa said. "Which doesn't feel very safe since we don't know what this place is."

Yat and Arakaki came over. Yat dared to walk out into the hexagon, stepping along one of the beams. Arakaki moved slightly more slowly, but otherwise she showed no distress.

"The door is here, set into the center," Yat said. Magnus took another look. He had not seen any evidence of a door at all. Yat's attendants sent back a feed of the center. Magnus saw a seam that indicated one of the central four-sided panels formed by the structural members was a portal.

"Good find! We're in business," Telisa said.

Magnus felt his legs shaking under the load.

"Wait. We may have to lose the packs," Magnus said.

"He's right," Arakaki said. "If we descend into there and get into trouble, climbing back up is going to be like carrying bars of gold out of a pit."

Telisa did not say anything for a moment as she thought it over.

"Okay, you three leave your Rovan packs up here. I'll wear mine and cover your escape if we get into trouble."

Magnus nodded and slipped off the Rovan pack. His situation went from desperate to uncomfortable. He separated his backpack from the flat Rovan module and put it back on.

So much better.

Yat and Arakaki left their Rovan packs beside the hexagon. They returned looking grateful.

"Let's get inside," Telisa said eagerly.

"Will do," Yat puffed. He stepped back and opened his backpack to bring out a wand. Yat swept the wand around the edges of the door, trying to elicit some response. When that did not work, he put the wand away and closed his eyes to concentrate on his PV.

Arakaki looked out over the rocks, scanning the horizon. Magnus passed the time doing the same on the opposite side. He tried to imagine any creature that could survive on this desolate world.

If something does live here, it's probably a rock-skinned beast that vomits lava and eats... I have no idea what it could eat.

The air outside his suit was thin. If exposed, any Terran would likely gasp a few ragged breaths and collapse. Magnus watched the rocks and gave a fraction of his attention to nearby attendant feeds. Nothing moved.

I should really be watching for rovlings.

He was certainly outfitted to combat the small Rovan helpers. His main weapon fired tiny projectiles from an ultra-high capacity magazine. The projectiles were designed to penetrate a rovling and disable it. They were just powerful enough for that task—and not much else. Under the stubby barrel sat a glue helix launcher. If they encountered anything else, the laser pistol at his left hip and the stun baton at his right would have to do.

"Got it. Opening now," Yat reported.

Magnus did not turn. Instead, he peeked at the feeds from attendants that shot into the portal. They entered an airlock spacious enough for five people—or one Rovan.

"Cycle them through and we'll follow," Telisa told him.

The outer door closed. Four attendants within flew out and started to map the interior. Two dimly lit rooms contained wall bins and rovling tubes. A giant robotic arm ran the length of one room. Magnus supposed it was for moving heavy cargo in or out of the facility.

"Put out your soldiers to guard this area. We're going in," Telisa said. Magnus nodded and sent his machines a signal. Eight of his six-legged soldier bots crept out of each shuttle and took up positions around the hexagonal platform. Once they were deployed, Magnus shifted his attention to the airlock. Yat had reopened it.

Telisa waved her hand in a circle and pointed down. The four PIT members carefully dropped into the lock to follow their attendants inside. It felt like a surrender to gravity.

Two attendants set off down rovling tubes and two more headed down a corridor that spiraled downward. Eventually the corridor formed a Y, giving them two options. The attendants split up, but both sides quickly met sealed doors.

"Choices, choices," Telisa said. "Let's go left."

"Actually, I think I can open these two doors through the attendants," Yat said. "We don't have to advance yet if you don't want to."

"Let's open one can of worms at a time. Tell the attendant to open the left side and we'll head down there."

Magnus emerged from the lock into the first Rovan room. The light levels were noticeably lower than he had experienced at the last Rovan complex. His suit notified him that the environment had become pressurized and the air was breathable.

"Open up?" Magnus asked.

"The attendants think it's safe to breathe," Telisa said. "Yes, go ahead."

Magnus told his faceplate to open. He tested the air.

"Musty. A little smelly, actually."

"Maybe water seeps in from the lake," suggested Arakaki.

Magnus examined the floor. It looked dirty. He thought it might be slimy but decided not to check other than seeing if his boots would slip. They seemed to retain good traction.

The heavy gravity was miserable. He found himself admiring Siobhan all the more for not constantly complaining about all the Earth-sized planets they had been on.

She was tougher than I realized. She said a few things here and there, but mostly she bore it.

He watched the left door open in an attendant feed. The attendant fearlessly accelerated into the unknown. It wandered through dark corridors, finding several more doors. It descended down a ramp to the next level of the facility.

"The place feels deserted," Magnus said.

"It might just be the darkness," Telisa commented. "I wonder if this is a night cycle and the lights will get brighter in sync with a standard Rovan day, whatever that's like."

"We never encountered that at the other Rovan buildings," Yat pointed out.

"Let's move. The attendants haven't found so much as a single rovling," Telisa said.

They slipped through the open door into the darkness. Their personal attendants illuminated the corridor around them. The team activated their weapon lights as well, providing plenty of light. Magnus saw the familiar red bars painted at intervals in the tunnels. Telisa led them to another door. She looked at Yat and pointed.

Yat approached the door and started the open sequence. Arakaki and Magnus kept their weapons ready and watched the corridors around them while Telisa prepared to go through the door.

The portal opened into a long, narrow corridor. Vertical pipes as thick as Magnus's upper legs ran from floor to ceiling at even intervals down the corridor. Magnus saw perhaps twenty of them in the Telisa's video feed. The ceiling was low.

No Rovan could get through here. Must have been a rovling access tunnel.

Telisa crouched and led the way forward. They padded through the narrow corridor in single file. At the end, an oval opening led into the next room. They stepped through the opening into a vast chamber. The far side was at least thirty meters distant, but the left-right length of the chamber ran even longer... farther than Magnus could make out past the torso-width pipes and truck-sized tanks that dominated the center. Magnus oriented himself on the map. To his right, the long part of the room extended toward the underground lake.

"Huge pipes. Huge tanks. Obvious enough. So where does the water go?" Arakaki asked.

"One of these pipes rises all the way to the hexagonal platform where we entered," Yat answered.

"So it's harvested and taken away!" Telisa concluded.

"This is nothing more than a water station?" Arakaki asked.

"Maybe," Telisa said. "Let's go back and check out the other branch."

The exploration team retraced their steps through the dim complex. Magnus imagined what it would have been like to explore these dark, dank corridors without the attendants scanning all around them.

Ancient explorers had immense courage.

Yat had an attendant waiting at the right door to begin the breaching process. They waited in single file for a minute until the door opened. The explorer attendant moved forward to start mapping and scout for danger. After a few seconds, Telisa and her attendants followed.

Magnus watched the team's flank and followed slowly. He caught up with Telisa in a long, dark room. Stacks of three-meter metal bars rose three quarters of the way to the eight-meter-high ceiling. Most were shades of silver; some gleamed whitely, others were almost black.

"Raw materials storage?" asked Arakaki.

"I'm guessing this has been mined from the meteorite," Telisa said.

The next room held vats, pipes, and crisscrossed struts linking it all together. A giant conveyor belt led up through two truck-sized machines and into a tunnel on the far wall.

"Looks like some kind of processing plant, a smelter or maybe a metal mill," Telisa said.

"It would be mostly iron, right? That's a poor material for making spacecraft. They must have wanted to build something here," Magnus said.

"Maybe, but it's a readily available local resource," Telisa said.

"Rovlings!" Yat announced sharply.

Arakaki and Magnus swept the room with their weapons, but no rovlings were visible. Then Magnus spotted three of them in the attendant feed from a hundred meters away. The rovlings were compact as before, but these machines had shorter, sturdier legs. A broad drill head lay atop each of their bodies. They moved in a steady, dull way.

"They're sluggish," Telisa noted.

"Possible signs of low energy conditions," Yat said. "Low lights, slow rovlings."

"Or a heavy gravity design. They don't need to move fast, anyway, right?" Arakaki asked.

"Who knows how old this station is? Hundreds of years? Thousands?" asked Magnus.

"You're right about the meteorite. These rovlings are mining the mineral deposits," Yat said, still accessing the attendants' feeds. "There are... maybe kilometers of tunnels ahead."

"I'll pass on going that way," Arakaki said.

"I agree," Magnus said. "If we go into those tunnels and get ambushed by the rovlings... it might be nightmarish getting out, even with our new weapons."

"Maybe they only have the drills," Telisa said. "I wonder how many it would take to break through one of our force field packs."

"Maybe there's a kind of balance here," Magnus said, changing the subject. "They're reducing the pressure bearing down on the lake by taking material away from the meteorite plate... and draining the water below."

"Maybe, but I'd expect if they take a lot of water from here, the ceiling would drop, or even collapse," Yat said.

"We don't need to calculate the structural dynamics of how the operation works," Telisa said dismissively. "The point is, this is a supply station. The important question is, who was it supplying with water and metal?"

Magnus could hear the frustration in her voice. The station was a little different than others they had seen, but this place offered no groundbreaking discovery. Just an army of ancient rovlings gathering minerals and a collection of huge tanks holding water supplies that probably had not been accessed in centuries.

"Got something!" Arakaki said. "One of the attendants detected vibrations behind a door over in the water section."

A machine left running?

"Probably another rovling," Yat said.

"We didn't see any rovlings wandering around on that side. It's worth a look," Telisa said.

They turned away from the mining tunnels and walked back to the first side they had investigated.

"I'll get it..." Yat said. After a moment, he looked perplexed. "Hrm."

Magnus waited for an explanation, but Yat said nothing. After a minute, the door still had not opened. Yat was deep into his PV.

"Active resistance?"

"No. But this door has been changed. It's a challenge."

Magnus and Telisa traded looks. They stood to either side of the door, on edge. Arakaki faced away from the door, down the corridor.

The door finally cycled open. Telisa's weapon came up and she stormed into the room. Magnus followed on her heels, ready for anything.

A huge brown corpse lay before them. The desiccated mass would have been difficult to identify if it had not been draped inside a massive Rovan shell.

"Yuck," Arakaki said, summing up the entire thing from the doorway. "A Rovan mummy."

"What the hell?" Yat murmured.

A scraping noise caught Magnus's attention. Telisa's reactions were faster. She had her weapon trained toward the sound in an instant. Magnus heard a crackling in the air as her force field came on. Yat and Arakaki faded out into stealthed ghost outlines.

A rovling skittered up the far wall. It was a normal, thin-legged rovling, not one of the thick, knobby-legged miners. Two more normal rovlings came around the other side of the corpse.

Pop. Snap. Pop. Zing.
Ka-Blam!

Telisa's weapon barked, shattering the first rovling across the far wall. Magnus activated his weapon and dropped to one knee so he would not obstruct her fire.

Ka-Blam!

Telisa obliterated the other two rovlings with one shot before Magnus's weapon fired. He advanced counterclockwise around the corpse, checking the rest of the room.

"Clear," he said.

Arakaki and Yat became visible again.

"I guess he had his personal retinue in here with him," Telisa said. "This shotgun works well enough. Killed those last two with one shot."

"What got 'em?" Arakaki asked, pointing at the defunct Rovan.

"Radiation, maybe," Yat guessed.

"Let the attendants get everything scanned before we take a sample. Maxsym will tell us," Telisa said.

Arakaki covered the door.

"It dried up," Magnus noted. "It was sealed in here. Must have been just the right conditions to preserve the body."

Three attendants swept all over, across, and through the huge shell and its dry contents. Then one of them paused to cut away a bit of it for analysis. Telisa stood staring at the dead hulk for few seconds.

Magnus noticed an attendant fell off their tactical. Then another within the second.

"Do you need backup for an extraction?" Barrai transmitted. "You've lost two attendants."

Damn. Here we go again.

Telisa she turned and headed for the door.

47

"No. We're on our way," Telisa said. "Magnus, send your soldiers in to block anything here, at the choke leading into those tunnels." She highlighted a spot on the tactical.

"You got it," he said. He sent the soldiers into the station. There were likely other paths around the choke, but Magnus hoped this would keep any rovlings from immediately cutting of their planned escape path.

"You're worried that the mining rovlings will attack as well?" Yat asked.

"I don't think they could take out attendants without ranged weapons, but let's not find out. Stealth up, on me," Telisa said.

Everyone winked out of sight to be replaced by their pale ghosts in Magnus's link-enhanced vision. A few steps later, the sounds of battle echoed through the passageway. The tactical showed his soldier machines trading fire with multiple types of rovlings: the miners charged forward to engage directly, while a handful of normal-looking rovlings sniped from the rear.

"Don't engage. It's not worth fighting a swarm of miners for this place," Telisa said.

"I'd kind of like to try out this weapon, too," Magnus said, breathing hard from the quick move out.

"Okay. When we come to the junction, pause. Magnus, give them a burst or two," Telisa said, surprising him. She did not have to offer twice; Magnus pressed the pace up to the junction where the action was.

In one quick scan he sized up the situation: At least twenty dead rovlings lay stacked in the corridor past five of his own machines that had fallen.

With his stealth active, he felt less need for cover. He knelt at the corner and brought up his weapon. Four enemy rovlings charged through the mess of their dead companions.

Ratatatatatat.

His tiny projectiles flew out and smacked into the rovlings. They halted, twitching and smoking.

"Works well," he summarized.

"Go go go," Telisa said.

The team double-timed it up the ramps to the entrance. The heavy gravity made itself felt in the most awful way. Magnus felt the burn in his legs as they ascended, until his suit released a chemical into his bloodstream that washed it away.

The tactical showed a new wave of miner-rovlings pressing Magnus's machines hard. Magnus frowned, but he satisfied himself with the thought there would be a lot of video to go through and analyze that could be used to improve his designs.

Yat and Arakaki were through the exit hatch first.

"Go," Telisa told him. He did not argue. Trilisk Special Forces would be the last out.

He emerged onto the surface with a hand from Yat. The shuttles were open and ready to receive them. Yat and Arakaki grabbed their Rovan packs, then staggered off to get into their shuttle. Magnus grabbed his own and huffed and puffed toward his shuttle.

Telisa bolted out of the Rovan station with superhuman speed and agility. She reached the shuttle ramp in a single bound, even in the higher gravity. Then the shuttle rose from the surface even as the doors closed.

Magnus deactivated his stealth. Telisa slammed into a seat next to him and followed suit.

"The facility beneath you has started to emit a repetitive EM signal," Barrai reported.

"Distress call," Telisa said.

"Likely," Marcant said.

"Does that help you learn anything more about their communications?" Telisa asked.

"One more piece of the puzzle," Marcant said.

"Barrai. What else have you got for us?" Telisa demanded.

"Nothing, TM," Barrai said curtly.

"What? Just this little place? Out here on a single rocky planet in an uninhabitable system?" Yat asked.

"No other facilities have been discovered," Barrai said. "We sent probes to the other planet as well. No luck."

"Okay, we're coming back up," Telisa said.

She looked as confused as Yat had sounded.

Magnus understood her reaction. Something felt wrong about a lone facility like this with a single Rovan. The place was too focused on mining to be a science base or a military complex. Yet it was too insignificant to be supplying water or ore to distant systems.

Could it have been an outpost designed to watch the system? Why? This place seems to be of no particular importance.

Magnus knew they would get to the bottom of it.

Chapter 6

Arakaki let out a long breath in the shuttle bay and forced herself to relax.

"Another day in the xeno mines," Yat said, dropping his heavy Rovan field pack to the deck.

"We should have brought those soldier robots in with us in the first place," Arakaki said. She dropped her pack and immediately felt the relief of shedding the burden. The Rovan packs were manageable in Earth gravity, but the rocky alien planet below had been too much.

Yat did not answer.

She fell in beside Yat and walked toward her quarters. A treaded Space Force robot picked up the packs behind them and set them upon its low, flat body. It started to recharge the force field packs as it trundled along behind Arakaki.

Arakaki enjoyed the silence and looked forward to resting.

"We have a Rovan starship inbound," Barrai announced.

Frag me.

"Damn!" Yat uttered aloud.

"Maxsym, get *Iridar* cloaked," Telisa ordered. "*Sharplight* will handle this."

"The distress call," Magnus said. "That ship had to have been in-system to get here this fast."

Either that, or the Rovans are a hell of a lot more advanced than we thought.

Arakaki reluctantly increased her speed. If she had to sit through trouble, she did not want to be out in the corridors.

"Does this happen to you guys all the time? It's awful," Yat said.

"Lots of ways to die in this universe," Arakaki replied.

"I mean, at least when you go into action on the ground, you have all your training behind you. But when the ship is threatened, we can only sit here and wait to see what happens."

They reached the corridor of their quarters.

"The others on the team train on this all the time. We rely upon them," Arakaki said.

"But if the ship is too big, too advanced—"

"We face the same danger on the ground. If we ran into a bunch of Trilisk soldier robots or something crazy like that, we'd be just as helpless."

They walked into her quarters. Arakaki put her weapons, orb, and claw into a locker built into the wall.

She received a crash tube warning. Yat looked at her. She stared back at him.

"Get into a crash tube," Yat urged.

"Let's wait and see what the situation is," Arakaki said.

"We can evaluate the situation from our crash tubes."

"If it's my time to go—"

"You have a reason to live now, idiot!" Yat exploded. He stomped over to a shelf extending from the wall. With an angry slap of his hand he sent her armor sliver necklace flying across the room.

"Forget about this stupid thing. You have a *new* life to live now. Get in the damn crash pod!" he yelled.

Arakaki stood, more stunned than she had been since serving as a green recruit in combat for the first time.

"They're attacking us," Barrai reported. "Energy draw on the shields and missiles incoming."

Arakaki snapped out of it.

"Okay," she said. Her crash tube opened and she headed for it. Yat ran out to find a tube of his own.

"Damage?" Telisa asked.

"*Sharplight* can handle it," Barrai said. "At this range, at least. We're charging rings to fire all point defenses."

Arakaki stepped into the tube and put her back against the rest. The cover slid shut without a sound. She lay nestled within the metal cocoon, more shocked by Yat than the sudden Rovan attack.

Didn't see that one coming.

The *Sharplight* trembled, ever so slightly. Arakaki's perspective finally shifted to the more pressing concern of their survival.

"I thought you said—" Telisa started.

"That was something else," Barrai said. "We have adequate power to take out these missiles and fire back."

"Then what was it?" Marcant asked.

"Get us out of here," Telisa ordered. "Make it clear we don't want to fight them. Maybe real Rovans are at the helm."

"Is it really wise to be target practice for them?" Marcant complained. "You're sure they can't hurt us?"

"We can hold off its energy weapons," Barrai confirmed. "It can't break through our shields."

Arakaki checked the ship to ship tactical. A pane in her PV showed her the relative positions of the ships. The *Sharplight* was turning away to keep several light seconds of distance between them.

She perused their data on the enemy. The Rovan ship massed less than one-third of the *Sharplight*.

The missiles had eaten up more than half the distance between the vessels. As Arakaki watched, the twenty points split into one hundred.

"That's bad," Marcant said.

"Not helpful, Marcant," Telisa said.

"It's actually good," Barrai said. "Those aren't large enough to have spinners of their own!"

The *Sharplight* accelerated on the tactical, though Arakaki could not feel it. Barrai was spooling up the gravity spinner. The missiles rate of closure dropped. It began to look like the *Sharplight* might pull away.

"The missiles are chatting with one another," Adair said mildly.

"Saying what?"

"I don't know, but I'm storing it for analysis."

"The ship is turning away," Barrai said. "It's headed back for the planet."

Arakaki saw it on the tactical. The missiles were still headed outward, but were no longer gaining on *Sharplight*.

"Good. They have no interest in pursuing us," Telisa said. She did not sound happy. Arakaki knew their leader was berating herself for getting on the bad side of the local Rovan forces again.

"We need to be able to talk to them," Telisa said.

"We're working on it, I promise," Adair said brightly.

"Can you at least say, 'we come in peace?'" Magnus asked.

"Maybe. Or maybe we'll be saying, 'we're here for your shells'."

"Keep me apprised," Telisa growled.

The tactical showed that the missiles had fallen back and failed to alter course as the *Sharplight* followed a slow arc around the system. Arakaki judged that the crisis was over. She told her crash tube to open.

Arakaki stripped off her Veer suit and headed across the room in her undersheers. As she put on some loose clothes, Yat came to the door. Arakaki swallowed and told it to let him in. When it opened, he walked in slowly.

"The last person to chew me out like that was a superior officer," she noted mildly.

"I'm sorry," Yat said. "I had no right—"

"I'm glad you care about me. It's okay you kicked my ass into the crash tube."

"What? I'm not apologizing about that! I'd do it again in a heartbeat! I was apologizing for knocking away your armor sliver and telling you to get rid of it."

Arakaki smiled. "Ah. I see. Well, sometimes certain hidden feelings only come out when we're angry. Or so it seems."

Yat shrugged.

"C'mon. I'm starving," she announced, pulling him by the hand. They left for the ship's mess.

Michael McCloskey

Chapter 7

Marcant was frustrated. So much Rovan data, so little they could discern from it.

He sighed.

It might as well be an endless pile of random numbers.

Marcant rubbed his eyes and lurched up from his VR chair. He stretched, then fell into a set of pushups.

"Look what the PIT team has done to me," he lamented to Adair. "I'm exercising! When perfectly good toning pills are just across the room."

"Poor jelly-brain has a jelly-body, too," Adair said. It pranced about Marcant's room as if showing off its new robotic body in comparison.

"Your body is creepy," Marcant said. "If I wake up in the middle of the night and see that... metal spider-thing, I'll probably conclude some alien has sent its robots to harvest my body."

"You'll get used to it," Adair said. Marcant supposed it was right.

"We need to check the rest of the system," Telisa announced on the PIT channel.

"'The rest'?" Marcant echoed. "There isn't much else to see out here. I mean the neutron star is spectacular with all that superheated material falling into it, but it's no Rovan base."

"That station was put here to mine minerals and water for something local," she said. "It isn't an interstellar mining operation. It's too small. Plus that small ship responded to the alert quickly. We're missing something here."

"And why was the base so well hidden?" Barrai asked.

"Well, if you were a Rovan, what's of interest here?" Magnus said.

"Maybe there's a science base that studied the neutron star," Maxsym suggested.

"That's good thinking," Telisa said. "Maybe there isn't a Rovan colony, just some Rovan presence that was noted in the data we stole. Where should we check—"

"Here are our possibilities," Barrai said, sending a pointer. "I would search the most distant but stable orbits of the neutron star, since that sounds good for a science base. Otherwise, we have triangular L4 and L5 points of the two stars to check."

Marcant agreed with the assessment. A distant orbit of both stars was also a possibility, but that was both less likely and also much more volume to search. If a passive object with low albedo hid out that far, it could take a year to find it.

"There's plenty of energy in this area to harvest. A dynamic path through the system is also possible," Adair said. "Still, the points Barrai suggest are good places to start."

I really believed there was a Rovan colony here, Marcant thought. *The data had to mean something... could it have been nothing more than an exploration plan?*

The hours marched on as the *Sharplight*'s probes searched the system. The starship followed the line of the general search, leaving the vicinity of the larger rocky planet and heading out into the vast space between the standard sequence star and the neutron star.

Marcant thought himself in circles. He told himself the Rovans would not be so dumb as to make a colony in this system. The binary had to be millions of years old. They could not have been 'surprised' by a rogue neutron star.

Marcant's monitoring programs brought an anomaly to his attention. He brought it up in his PV. A probe nearing the L5 zone had found two artificial objects drifting there.

Barrai was getting the same feed. "We've found something at a stable point here," she reported on the PIT channel.

"Take us there," Telisa ordered.

The probes showed two fat, top-shaped stations, each nearly a kilometer in diameter with a center spine that ran almost the same distance. Their tails pointed toward the neutron star.

"They're embedded at the neutron-star side of the stable zone," Adair pointed out. Marcant knew what that meant.

"They have gravity spinners active for local comfort. The resulting pull on the station is being balanced against the neutron star's pull," he summarized.

"I think so," Adair said. "The math works out for an equilibrium in the neighborhood of a standard gee, depending on how the spinner is focused. If I had to guess, I'd say they're a little on the heavy side."

Marcant recalled the thick legs of the Rovans. They could well have evolved on a planet with slightly higher gravity than Earth provided.

"The absorption signatures are similar to the other ships we've encountered," Barrai said.

"The Rovan ships," Arakaki clarified.

"Presumed Rovan," Telisa corrected. "We'll know soon enough."

Marcant perused the scans of the stations. He noted general radial symmetry in the body of the station. Engineering sections ran along the center and through to the tail. The station emitted light from dozens of ports.

"We need an attendant out there to sneak up and take a peek though those ports," Marcant said on the PIT channel.

"Yes," Telisa agreed. "As we match course and spool down the spinner, let's release a couple."

"Not a colony... but these are major stations," Marcant thought aloud.

"Bigger than I would expect any science base to be," Adair added.

"I'm itching to know what the Rovans were doing out here," Telisa said on the team channel.

"I'm going to go out on a limb and say it had to do with the decision to leave the other colony," Magnus said.

"Really?" Maxsym asked. "Why do you have such a belief?"

"That planet was fine. The Rovans abandoned it. I think it was a strategic withdrawal in the face of an enemy. I think these stations are here because their enemy would not think to look for them in this system."

"Pure supposition," Marcant said.

"I see no evidence of any weaponry on these stations," Barrai said. "That doesn't support your theory, Magnus. If I made a hidden base here in time of war, it would be heavily armed."

"I'm glad they have no armament. I want to learn what they are without being shot at," Telisa said.

Marcant waited impatiently for the *Sharplight* to approach the L5 zone. Finally, they closed to a fraction of

a light second and released two attendants. The tiny
Vovokan machines shot off to take a close look.

Marcant accessed a view from the lead attendant, got
one second of the feed as the orb passed the last kilometer
of distance, then the feed stopped.

"Blocked!" Barrai said.

"What?" Magnus asked.

"The lead attendant just vaporized," Barrai said.

"A force field, of course," Arakaki supplied.

"Yes. The first attendant was destroyed at point blank
range, within the last hundred meters. I'm slowing the
other," Marcant said.

The huge base dominated the feed of the second
attendant. Marcant brought it in to the point where the first
attendant died, slowing the spy machine to one meter per
second. The view stabilized. Marcant could see from the
numbers in his PV that the range was not closing.

"It's stuck there," Marcant told them. "It's not being
harmed, but it's not able to get any closer."

"Is there any evidence the bases are manned?" Telisa
asked. "I don't see anything from the probes."

"Nothing," Maxsym said. "I can't see any indication
there are live Rovans aboard."

Telisa sighed.

"We'll try communication first," she announced. "If
that fails, and if we still have no indication there are any
live Rovans or AIs there, we need to analyze the design of
these bases and see if we could breach the shields and take
out the generators without destroying the stations."

Marcant understood Telisa's position. She hated the
idea of breaking into bases and space stations, possibly
causing even more Rovan animosity, but she refused to

just leave the discoveries behind when they had reason to believe the Rovans were long gone.

"Adair, can you work with Yat on the communications angle? I want to see if Marcant can figure out a clever way of detecting Rovans over there, assuming the communications fail again."

"Thank you for your confidence," Adair said.

"I'm on it," Marcant said.

The first idea Marcant had to check for Rovans would be to listen for radio chatter, or any evidence of data being transferred to and from each station, especially between them. As he threw together a program for that investigation, he kept thinking: how else could he tell?

Marcant ticked off what living Rovans would need to survive.

Heat. Pressure. Air. Food.

A thermal analysis would likely reveal if the station was widely heated or shut down. If it was pressurized, there might be microscopic leakage through the hull that extremely sensitive instruments could detect. The force screen would not help, though.

He thought beyond those requirements. He had listed what they needed to live; if they had those things, as a consequence of living there would be side effects. Surely the Rovans did not sit still like statues all day long? They must move. That would cause vibrations. Those vibrations would not carry through space (and maybe not the force field, either), but vibrations could be detected with sensitive enough optical study or Vovokan mass sensors on the *Iridar*. What else?

The center of mass of the station would change. The gravitational attraction between our ship and theirs would fluctuate by the tiniest amounts.

Satisfied that he had a good list of approaches to try, he got to work.

He set up the analyses, commandeered a probe, and scheduled some time slots with the *Sharplight*'s sensors to gather data. The thermal analysis was easy. The body of the station was heated, the spine less so. His quick take on that was that the round body must be where the living things resided, and the spine was for other systems that could be maintained by robots.

Yat and Adair were chatting on the team channel, exchanging ideas and reporting to Telisa. Marcant half-listened only so that he would know if they succeeded in contacting a live Rovan.

Marcant found that the force field was too far removed from the surface of the station for him to tell if air was leaking out. His probes would have to be centimeters away to detect a few stray molecules shooting out of it. The good news was that he could visually pick up fluctuations in the hull. It was vibrating, but he did not know how to interpret the data he was receiving.

Marcant recruited the mass sensors of the *Iridar* and told the Vovokan ship to approach to take readings with its mass sensors. While that happened, he had an attendant scan the *Sharplight* to learn about what was causing their hull to vibrate and how much of that energy was caused by the crew.

It's challenging, of course... though if I learn how to do this and keep the programs around, it may be useful again later.

Marcant's processes identified sources of vibration within their own ship. He started masking them out, looking for Terran footsteps. Many obstacles clouded his view; the hull vibrations varied in so many ways. The footsteps could be light or heavy, near or distant from the hull, and if the alien hull was stiffer or more elastic than their own, everything would shift. Marcant had to make many adjustments.

As Marcant worked, other results came in. He discovered that the center of mass of the station had drifted over time. The effect was small; so small that he wondered if it could be explained by changes in radiation pressure. The *Iridar* reported masses moving within the ship, but the signatures were too small to be Rovan.

Probably just rovlings moving in there.

"It's a big decision to shoot at that ship," Telisa was saying.

"We don't have to shoot the ship itself," Barrai said. "I could hit the forcefield hard on a line to miss the ship, then, before the shield recovers we could send attendants through."

"I like it. I wish we knew if these stations are still active."

"Something *is* moving over there," Marcant asserted. He enjoyed being the one to deliver that information more than strictly necessary. "The source of that movement is unknown to me, though I think it's more of those robotic rovlings. I've been working on a way to try and detect heavy footfalls over there, like those a Rovan might make, but I can't be sure, even with *Sharplight*'s amazing optical sensors. There are a lot of unknowns, like how stiff that hull is, where they might be inside, how heavy their footfalls would be..."

"Keep trying, everyone," Telisa said. "I don't want to—"

"We have a new contact," Barrai said. "It's on the map."

Marcant checked. The new discovery had a Rovan signature and it was bigger than the patrol ship that had come to the mining station.

"There's another one!" Marcant announced.

"It's way out of position if it's a station," Yat noted.

"It's falling toward the neutron star!" Marcant said.

"I can verify that," Barrai said. "It has gained a lot of velocity relative to the star."

"What is it? A ship?" Telisa asked.

"The parts of its exterior we can observe are almost identical to these two bases," Barrai said.

"Barrai, can we save it?" Telisa asked.

"Yes, the *Sharplight* can do it," Barrai said. "Though there's not much room for error."

"Then let's get started," Telisa said. "We're not going to let one of our three clues slip away."

Michael McCloskey

Chapter 8

Barrai sat in a hefty chair in a command lounge at the center of the *Sharplight*. Many Space Force personnel liked to call such chairs "command thrones" after the term appeared in a famous comedy of the last century called *On Safari with High Lord Kre*. Marcant had a similar rig in his quarters; they were built to support a person engrossed in online work for days if necessary.

I have my work cut out for me.

At Barrai's control, *Sharplight* accelerated toward the distant target before the computers had formulated a complete course plan. If it was going to be a close thing, there was no time to waste and she knew the general direction of the mission.

The alien station was not generating any thrust. The probes told Barrai that external forces pulled it toward the neutron star. The star held well over two solar masses of dense material. Though there was no event horizon above its surface, the star was dangerous to operate around.

The *Sharplight* could only tow ships by putting them under the influence of its gravity spinner, and since the warship was not designed for towing this way, there were severe limitations on how much pull it could exert on another ship. Luckily, warships produced a lot of a critical component: power.

A query she had fired off finished. The *Sharplight* had found a configuration allowing the *Iridar* to contribute to the operation.

"Maxsym, I'm enlisting the help of the *Iridar*," Barrai said.

"Uhm... if you must?" Maxsym said nervously.

"In the Vovokan ship, you'll be safer than we are," Telisa assured him.

"I'll find a crash pod," the scientist said.

Barrai estimated that Telisa's statement was correct, but probably not by as much as she thought. Without careful coordination, using both spinners to pull the alien station could result in disaster.

The first course plans and procedures came through. Barrai enabled the recommended one and started to review the alternates. She shut down several nonessential systems in order to route power into temporary storage rings so that they would have power to spare for whatever occurred.

"Tube it if you got it," Barrai rattled off, warning the team to seek crash tubes. "Dilating our spinner field to maximum radius. The *Iridar* is mirroring us across this plane."

The spinner diagram threw up a transparent plane through the middle of the target station. The *Iridar* approached in an identical manner reflected across the plane. The smaller Vovokan ship struggled to match the power output of *Sharplight*; Barrai's protocols dropped the *Sharplight*'s spinner to match up.

"Fifty thousand kilometers," Barrai said. The spinners' interactions were becoming significant. She had them matched up perfectly.

I hope the stubborn among us found their crash pods, Barrai thought.

A slight tremor ran through the ship.

What's that?

Notification panes flashed red in her PV. Barrai absorbed the warnings rapidly.

"Bad news," she said on the PIT channel. "That station's spinner hasn't given up the ghost just yet. It's still intermittently kicking in and out."

"Could it be doing it on purpose?" Magnus asked. "Warning us off?"

"I don't think so," Barrai said. "There are clearer ways to signal that... but they are aliens."

"No, it's no warning," Adair said. "Think over the facts: that station clearly doesn't belong out here this close to the neutron star. Its spinner has been failing for a long time and it's in its death throes."

"Help me out here," Telisa said. "If their drive flares up when we're close, does that mean we won't be able to match up?"

"That's right," Magnus said. "They'll break us up just as surely as a ship choosing the Pirate's Option over capture by the Space Force."

"But this ship is so much more powerful," Yat said.

"That helps, but it's not going to cut it," Barrai told them. "That station is big. That little tremor we felt would have been a catastrophic shear at close range. And we can't pull them without getting a hell of a lot closer."

Another, stronger tremor rattled the ship as if to accentuate Barrai's warning.

"I'm holding us at thirty thousand kilometers," she said. "Sit tight, Maxsym. You okay over there?"

"My teeth are rattling, *Sharplight*," Maxsym said.

"Any other options worth considering?" Telisa asked.

"I recommend a surgical strike to that station's spinner," Barrai said. *Sharplight*'s weapons-targeting systems scanned the alien station, analyzing the gravity field gradients to calculate possible shots into the source spinner. New PVs sprang open in her mind, showing possible targets.

"That won't cause a catastrophic explosion?" Arakaki asked.

"Well, it might. But ninety percent, no," Barrai said.

"And what kind of chances are we looking at if we don't make the strike?" Telisa said.

"Worst case scenario, the spinners are damaged so severely that all three ships fall into the neutron star. In pieces. We could mitigate by leaving the *Iridar* out of this. That simplifies the match up and reduces the damage the Rovan spinner could cause, but we lose the *Iridar*'s extra strength. I'm not sure we can pull it by ourselves without getting *really* close."

"Prepare to fire," Telisa said. "There are two other stations back there we can investigate, and if we damage this one, it's still better than letting it fall into the star."

Thank the Five this TM has some sense, Barrai thought.

Targeting solutions came through. Barrai needed that energy she had stashed away now; the ship's weapons prepared to take a long drink of it.

"Ready to fire. Here we go."

Energy lanced out from the *Sharplight* into the void and sliced completely through the Rovan station. A small cloud of debris spread from the target, but it held together. Barrai's PV showed her that the flickering gravity field of the station stabilized at mass-normal.

"Got it," Barrai said. "If it looks like it's not gonna blow, we can resume our close-in within the minute."

"Good job," Telisa said. "Hear that, Maxsym? You and the *Iridar* are still in this!"

"Ah, thank you very much," Maxsym said. His voice did not quaver but he sounded miserable.

Barrai smiled. Poor Maxsym. He was stunningly brilliant, just not cut out for the rough edges of their missions. Barrai thought of their last sparring session. She would toughen him up yet.

The alien station showed no signs of instability. Its spinner was undoubtedly dead, but Barrai had a different doubt.

What if it has a backup? Nah. It wouldn't have slipped out of the safe zone if it did.

"Resuming the rendezvous," Barrai reported. The *Sharplight* and the *Iridar* moved in on the station on mirror courses.

Barrai thought about what else could go wrong. She looked the station over in their scans. It did not appear to have any weapons...

She allocated an energy storage unit to a weapons battery and locked it onto the Rovan station.

Just in case I have to hit it again.

Their target slowed relative to the neutron star as they put it into a stronger and stronger part of the combined spinner fields from the *Sharplight* and the *Iridar*. As they reached eight thousand kilometers between each ship, the station passed equilibrium and reversed course. Barrai moved in even closer until she was certain the configuration would be stable and efficient.

"Okay, we have it locked in. Everybody tug," Barrai said playfully. She felt truly alive. She watched her datapanes carefully. "We're winning!"

"Any reaction from the station, or the ones we left behind?" Telisa asked.

"Nothing," Adair replied immediately.

Adair must be watching them carefully. Makes sense. I've got my hands full with this.

Barrai remained vigilant. She noticed that Adair had recruited the sensors of both ships and some attendants to sweep the zone between the ships, looking for any anomalies.

It's making sure we don't collect any unwanted stowaways from that station, Barrai thought. *Those damn rovlings are a pain in the ass.*

Barrai remained focused on the operation and eased the three ships along. The time passed quickly as she concentrated on her work. After two hours of managing the tow operation, Barrai decided the hardest part was over.

"We have it. I'm contracting our fields back, then we can pull *Iridar* out of this. *Sharplight* can take it from here," Barrai reported.

"Thank you," Maxsym said. "And well done."

"Yes, excellent work," Telisa said. "This will be immensely helpful. Note that our runaway here doesn't have any shields up. We can learn what these stations do without having to shoot our way in!"

"Well, technically, we already shot it up," Marcant said.

"Oh, come on, shooting it to save it doesn't count," Barrai protested.

"I suppose not," Marcant agreed.

Chapter 9

Maxsym looked at the three backpacks he had prepared for the expedition onto the alien station they had saved.

Do I have everything? I could do with another sample and container pack. Maybe one of Magnus's robots could carry it...

"Maxsym, we're waiting on you," Telisa said.

"Sorry, headed that way. Magnus, could you send a robot to carry a pack for me? I want more sample containers and extra—"

"Come now," Magnus said. "I'll send a robot to grab your pack and take it to the bay. If we really need it that bad, we'll send for it."

"Right. Good idea," Maxsym said, dashing out the door of his lab. His Veer suit ran a diagnostic and reported full readiness as he lugged his three packs down the corridor. He reviewed what they had learned of the station in the last few hours.

The team called this station "S3" since it was the third they had detected in the binary system. No other artificial objects had turned up in any of the other places they thought to look, though probes still roamed throughout the system on vast search patterns. The station had power, so that was apparently not the cause of the spinner failure. No evidence of living Rovans had been found. The attendants had peeked into viewports but had not spotted any rovlings.

S3 rested only ten kilometers from *Sharplight*. The kilometer-wide station had a thick hull to help protect the interior from the radiation emanating from the neutron star as it dined on the system's dust and debris. It had no energy screens like S1 and S2 had; presumably those systems were damaged or simply exhausted. Attendants had entered through the hull breach created when *Sharplight* took down their spinner and found a few rooms now opened to the void. There were no Rovan corpses or artificial rovlings in the sundered rooms.

Maxsym did not know what to expect, but it would be interesting to learn what kind of a station S3 had been.

He loped into the shuttle bay. He could tell the others had been waiting too long. They watched him approach impatiently. Magnus and Telisa lounged against a Terran shuttle's landing gear. Arakaki and Yat sat side by side at the bottom of a deployed Vovokan shuttle ramp.

Maxsym felt a stab of disappointment. It seemed that Arakaki had chosen Yat. Maxsym chastised himself for not pursuing a relationship earlier; it was just that he had not thought Arakaki would ever notice him. Now he knew it was too late.

"Sorry, sorry," he told them.

The others seemed to accept his apology, as no one cast him an angry glance as they rose and jumped aboard. Maxsym hauled his supplies up into the shuttle. The hatch closed and they were underway within the minute.

"Why have we decided to go in this? Can *Sharplight* not dock with the alien station?" Maxsym asked.

"I made the call," Telisa told him. "I don't want to risk any hostiles getting aboard the *Sharplight*," she explained.

Maxsym nodded.

"That makes sense, though I admit I'm surprised. We have our new weapons, and Magnus has dozens of—"

"A hundred so far," Magnus corrected him.

"A hundred soldier machines designed to fight them," Maxsym finished.

"That station is huge. Who knows what's in there?" Barrai piped in through the PIT channel.

"Exactly. No need to risk our main ships," Telisa said. "We'll emerge amid twenty soldier robots on the surface of that station. If we're attacked, we'll bug out."

"Your landing site is clear," Barrai reported.

"Watch yourselves. Zero-g environment, thanks to Barrai's overzealous use of ship's weapons," Telisa said. She winked.

"That's cold, TM," Barrai replied in mock hurt.

Maxsym told his Veer suit to activate the magnetic clamps in his boots. His attendants would always be able to nudge him around if he went floating off, but Maxsym did not want to take a space walk. His Veer helmet extended over his head and dropped an airtight visor over his face.

The shuttle settled on the outer hull of the Rovan station.

The ramp extended and everyone hustled out. They were all used to zero-g and space ops because of their extensive VR training; even Maxsym exited gracefully and met the surface of the alien station without difficulty.

"It's all yours, Yat," Telisa said, pointing in the direction of the hatch they had targeted. The hatch was about four meters wide—large enough for a Rovan. About twelve hatches had been located in the hull; five of them were as big as this one. The rest were rovling-sized portals.

Yat approached the lock and started to work. Maxsym looked out over the surface of the station. It was dark and mostly smooth, though occasionally broken by depressions for hatches or extensions of hardware. The thought that it had been created by an alien intelligence still boggled his mind. What would it be like to talk with a Rovan? Would he ever find out?

"Open," Yat announced.

"Attendants and soldier bots," Telisa prompted. Four of Magnus's robots marched over and obediently entered the portal, accompanied by four attendants. The PIT team hung low on the skin of the station while the robotic vanguard cycled through to the interior.

Maxsym's training told him to keep an eye on his real surroundings as he watched the video feeds from their scouts within; in this case he doubted the utility of it since he simply stood on the surface of a station in the vacuum of space. He was glad that the body of the station obstructed the radiation emanating from the vicinity of the neutron star.

The lock opened into a prep room. Yellow walls were lit from one side by glowing panels. Maxsym told his link to adjust the feed so that the illuminating wall was considered to be the ceiling. Two half-meter thick red lines banded the room, crossing walls, floor, and ceiling. Rovling tubes emptied into the room on left and right at floor level.

The lead robot hesitated, then crossed the first red band. Nothing untoward occurred, so it forged on. The attendants shot on ahead.

There were no huge space suits evident; Maxsym wondered if Rovans ever went out into space since they could always send rovlings instead. The prep room had a single exit leading to a dark T intersection with a Rovan-sized corridor. The attendants peeled off in each direction, lighting the area around them with searchlights.

"Rovling tubes, but no rovlings," Yat noted.

"None we can see yet," Arakaki corrected him.

Maxsym watched the feed from one of the attendants. The view changed at a dizzying pace as the attendant dodged into a rovling tube, zipped sharply right and left with turns in the tube, and emerged into a long room filled with clear tanks of fluid. The lighting was minimal. The searchlights revealed one silver, two red, and several clear tubes or cables rising into each tank from the bottom.

The attendant flew past the row of tanks, then dipped to the floor and rose to the ceiling to get a full view of the room. Then it hurtled into the next room. Maxsym saw more rows of containers, though this time, the clear-walled containers were empty. He saw lights on the top and vents in the bottom of each unit.

Do those hold samples? Living things? Sick Rovans?

Maxsym noted that each of the chambers in the rooms were the same size and equipped identically, suggesting that these were not holding cells for unknown life or science experiment stations. They were all built to do the same thing, a job with known parameters.

"It's so strange that there's no rovlings here," Yat said.

"Maybe they're powered down," suggested Magnus. "The station was having a crisis."

"We didn't see them anywhere," Arakaki noted.

"There's probably a storage area that we can only get to through the tubes," Magnus said.

"The attendants have gone through any place the rovlings could travel," Marcant said. "Though we still have a lot of ground to explore, I think they moved the rovlings and who knows what else over to the other stations when the spinner on this one went bad."

"Let's hope they didn't move *all* the good stuff," Telisa said. "Follow me."

The PIT team entered the station's lock. Everyone except Maxsym cradled their weapons. To Maxsym, it felt like another of their VR training exercises.

If nothing goes wrong, it will feel weird, he realized. Something always went wrong in their exercises, though one never knew if it would be immediate or delayed.

"Perhaps some of our training exercises should go smoothly," he suddenly said.

"Why... ah, I think maybe I see what you mean," Telisa said. "We're trained to expect the worst, so much so, we're not really prepared for everything to go well!"

The conversation did not take off. Everyone waited alertly as the lock cycled and opened. Telisa led the way deeper into the Rovan station. Maxsym absorbed his first impression of the dark interior. The yellow room was clean and simple. Its size made him feel like a small pest wandering into the lair of a giant. His attendants carried him along so that he would not have to push off against anything unfamiliar.

Maxsym checked the air. "We can breathe here," he announced.

"Okay with me," Telisa said. "Keep clear of anything that could impede your helmet deployment in case we cause a breach."

Maxsym told his suit helmet to retract. He took a breath of cold air.

"The life support systems must be turned down," Yat said.

Magnus and Arakaki went in as if they were breaching a hostile facility, despite the fact that the forward attendants had seen zero resistance thus far. Their weapons' lights moved sharply back and forth. Telisa looked more relaxed but alert. He wondered how much more information her heightened senses were providing. Maxsym hung back and paid more attention to the feeds coming in.

What part of the station to check first?

Maxsym found a chamber on the map he found promising. It was an octagonal room, at least twenty meters wide, filled with intriguing machines. The tactical showed Magnus and Arakaki taking the lead in opposite directions from the initial T intersection.

"Permission to split up?" Arakaki asked.

"Granted," Telisa said.

Arakaki and Yat went left at the T. Magnus and Telisa took the right corridor. The rapidly expanding tactical map brought home the size of the station. There were many places the attendants could not go, but the countless tunnels being mapped were intimidating.

Maxsym decided to stick with someone else, at least for now. As the odd man out, he went right after Telisa and Magnus. It would be more comfortable to be with them. They proceeded fifty meters along a gentle curve, guided by the tactical map. He found the yellow corridor curious. A thick red line had been placed around the entire corridor every few meters. He stopped to press his finger against the outer wall. The yellow surface gave a millimeter or two, but it felt like a solid wall lay behind it.

Insulation? Ah! Perhaps an advanced kind of radiation shielding. That could be very interesting. It's obviously not dense...

Maxsym checked the conductivity with a probe. Then the inductivity. Both were low.

If the material has no free electrons, it shouldn't block radiation... need more tests.

His attendants nudged him on, catching him up to the other two. They had disappeared into a hatch on his left. Maxsym entered the smaller chamber. He caught sight of Telisa ahead in the low light.

The room had a soft floor. A facsimile of a Rovan stood in one corner. Each of its shell ports had an electrical connection assembly.

"Crazy," Marcant said. "A fake Rovan with charging stations for fake rovlings," he said.

"It looks cartoonish," Telisa mused. "You know what? It's for children."

"I have no better theory," Maxsym said.

Telisa and Magnus moved on. Maxsym hesitated, then noticed a hatchway leading upward to another level. He contacted Marcant.

"Entrance assistance, please? This one."

"Got it," Marcant said.

"Are you coming?" Magnus called.

"I see something interesting on the level above. I'm going to check it out," Maxsym said.

"Stick with the attendants and soldiers. Be cognizant of anything that might block a quick exit," Telisa ordered.

The tactical showed the room beyond, but it had been mapped by an attendant that had traveled through a rovling tube.

The door slid open.

Maxsym pushed into the octagonal room and let himself drift. A massive bank of machinery dominated the center, leaving about three meters of walkway around the perimeter. Several squarish modules with thick doors might be row of cold storage bins. Though alien, several things looked familiar: pipes running through each container, thick insulated hatches, and stubby legs holding the modules up off the floor.

"Heads up everyone, we just lost an attendant. No idea how," Telisa said.

"Maxsym, Yat, stay put. Magnus, send four soldier machines in there," Telisa ordered.

Maxsym looked around the room one more time, searching for threats he might have overlooked. He did not see any obvious robots or weapons ports.

He checked the tactical. Three attendants patrolled nearby in addition to his two personal ones that nudged him around in the zero-g. He called one of the free attendants and told it to join his other two guardians.

Maxsym returned his attention to the modules beside him. He examined one of the thick doors about the size of his chest. At first he found no manual levers or controls. He was about to call Marcant for help when he thought to look lower.

Maybe the active station had gravity pulling that way and rovlings wandered under there...

He found a series of switches and releases. Maxsym told his Veer suit to deploy his helmet to isolate himself from the environment. Then he cautiously flipped a latch guard on either side of the door. A glowing red bar appeared across a black panel on the front. The unit made a flat, snapping noise.

Locked? Or under pressure? Ah. The station lost some pressure when we breached the hull to take out the spinner.

Maxsym stepped to one side to clear the door. If it popped open too forcefully, he did not want to be injured. He told his attendants to bring him level with the floor so that his arm could use the controls from a safe spot.

This time, a loud hiss announced the release of the door. It came open a few centimeters.

"Lost one of the soldiers!" Marcant said.

"But now I know what's happening. See that? A laser emplacement."

Maxsym paid just enough attention to see that the area they spoke of was far away from his location. There were no enemies on the tactical, either. The two unattached attendants still patrolled the spaces around the room he occupied.

"I'm investigating a find here," Maxsym asked. "Should I deploy my grenades into the rovling tubes?"

"Still no evidence of rovlings, but go ahead, Maxsym. Better safe than sorry!" Telisa said.

Maxsym gave his two grenades rovling target sigs and sent them off. They each magnetized, attached to the floor, and rolled off toward a rovling tube.

With that, Maxsym refocused on the opened container. He told an attendant to widen the opening and oriented himself to get a better look.

A dozen rows of clear vials lay within. They had been kept secure in a white holder with an eight by eight array of holes. He grasped a vial with thumb and forefinger and pulled. It came out with a light resistance. A pinkish fluid rolled within the vial.

Maxsym checked it with his bioscanner.

"Potryasayushchi!"

"What? Oh," Magnus said as his link supplied a translation.

"Uhm. It's amazing. These contain globs of alien tissue!" Maxsym explained.

"What?"

"Rovan cells, perhaps. I've found a storage area with tissue. I don't know—actually I think I *do* know. These could be Rovan zygotes! This might be the prize I had hoped to find at the colony."

"That would explain why they hid these stations in this improbable system," Telisa said. "They had enemies as Magnus theorized. This may be their attempt to preserve their species."

"Interesting possibility," Marcant said from the *Sharplight*. "But you have no verification that's what they are yet, right?"

"We'll know soon. Magnus, I'll need that extra container after all."

"Okay. We're busy with these internal defenses at the moment, but I can arrange for it."

At this point, Maxsym could not imagine making any greater find. Whatever the Rovan laser emplacement protected, it probably would not interest him as much as these samples.

He noted the vial's temperature and put it back into the storage container for the time being. Then he unpacked his containers and thought about what he could bring back with proper temperature control. The lack of acceleration made it much more difficult to stay organized. There were several other storage units around him. He decided to first take stock of the others and see if their contents were the same.

He opened the next container just as carefully and found contents identical to the first, though it held twenty four vials. He continued and found the containers in various states of depletion, though each one had at least a handful of vials left.

"These bots will charge in. Then we'll hit it with our long range weapons," Magnus was saying on the PIT channel.

"Lost another one," Telisa noted.

Maxsym checked their feeds often enough to see that they were coordinating with the soldier bots to take out the emplacement without endangering themselves.

"Got it!" Magnus declared.

"Nice shot!" said Arakaki.

"Emplacement destroyed," Barrai said.

"Let's find out what's past that door!" Marcant declared.

Maxsym finally shifted his attention fully to the endeavors of his teammates a couple hundred meters away. Soldier robots proceeded past the destroyed laser emplacement at the center of the ship.

"Wait!" Maxsym burst out.

"Yes?" Telisa asked.

"What if it's booby trapped? Let me get these samples out into the shuttle first."

"You're going to run away *now* because of some vague fear of a trap?" started Arakaki.

"No. I wasn't planning on leaving the ship myself. These samples are *important*. If we die, at least Terra will have them."

"Okay, send them out, we'll hold for fifteen," Telisa said.

The channel was quiet for a minute, then Barrai decided to chat. "What do you think so far, TM?" she asked.

"Think about the childlike Rovan facsimiles we found, and the tissue samples Maxsym dug up. These walls are padded! I think this main deck is a giant nursery. They grow new Rovans here at the center. The farther from the center you get, the rooms are designed for bigger and bigger Rovans!" Telisa declared.

She's so observant! Could she be correct?

Maxsym checked their map. The rooms near the center were small with small doorways. The yellow padding Maxsym had noted was thicker near the center of the stations. The rooms expanded with the relative radius of their spot in the circular station. The portal sizes and sophistication grew along with the size.

"If that's right, I'd say there were roughly four stages here," Arakaki said. "Each stage has two or three rooms along any radial line before graduating to the next stage."

"The layout feels more like a factory than a nursery," Yat said.

"Maybe they were dying off and had to go for quantity," Arakaki said.

"Or it could be that this is the Rovan way. A child factory."

"They must have failed," Magnus said.

Maxsym considered Magnus's conclusion. Given all they had found, Magnus might be right.

Magnus's machines arrived to accept Maxsym's samples. He worked hurriedly, aware that he was holding up the team for the second time. Once the machines marched out, he retrieved his grenades and left for the others' position.

Maxsym stopped about twenty meters behind the others when the robots put the samples on a shuttle and left S3.

"They're clear," Maxsym reported, though the others were likely watching everything.

"Move in," Telisa ordered.

Maxsym watched the team's flank as they passed by the dead emplacement. There were still attendants moving through the station, searching for signs of rovlings, but Maxsym had been VR training with the team for a long time. He was seldom a part of any frontal assault, which left him with other responsibilities such as covering their backs.

He glimpsed at a feed from the front in his PV. Attendants and soldiers had moved through a hatch and into a series of tight hallways. The attendant feeding the view slowed.

"I feel heavy," Magnus said.

"Uhg. Feel that?" Arakaki said at the same time. "I feel faint."

"Back out of here," Telisa ordered.

"What's going on?" Marcant demanded.

"Something's dragging things in there," Telisa said. "See the attendants? They're affected, too."

86

"So not poison gas?" Maxsym asked. An attendant inside did not sense any change in the atmosphere.

"It's a kinetic dampening field," Barrai said.

"What? Rovan technology?"

"The Space Force has these," Barrai told them. "Though this one is stronger. It helps to prevent random disturbances that would destabilize energy states in molecular computers. It's only done for things like... is Yat cleared to hear this?"

"Yes," Telisa said.

"Things like the Avatar battle modules."

"I had no idea. Vovokan computers don't need this," Telisa pointed out.

"Vovokan hardware is a whole different world," Marcant said. "The Vovokan approach is more like... a swarm of crappy computers instead of a few buffed overdotted ones."

"The network is complex," Yat reported. "It does support the idea that those are sophisticated computers."

"There's also a massive datastore in there," Adair said.

"Maybe there will finally be some answers for us, then," Telisa said brightly.

Maxsym certainly hoped so, but three minutes later Marcant dashed those hopes.

"It's been wiped," he announced. "Either the defenses destroyed our prize, or the Rovans wiped it when they left."

Maxsym felt bad for that, but from his point of view, the prize was on the shuttle, already on the way back to his lab on the *Iridar*.

Michael McCloskey

Chapter 10

Yat stood behind Arakaki with his hands on her shoulders. The rest of the PIT team arrayed themselves nearby, eager to start investigating one of the active Rovan stations. He focused on Telisa when it became clear she was about to start.

"Here's the plan," Telisa said. "We're going to probe S1. This is an intelligence gathering mission. We'll insert some machines on the station and spy on it. Of course, we all want to find out if there are living Rovans over there, adults or juveniles. I also want to know if the rovlings on S1 and S2 are armed, how many of them there are, and how they react to intruders."

Telisa shared a pointer to a feed from a VR exercise. Yat accessed the feed and watched along as Telisa continued.

"Because the active stations have force fields, we'll use Barrai's itchy trigger finger to temporarily suppress the fields and slip a stealthed shuttle through."

The simulation showed the *Sharplight* firing energy beams through the station's defensive screens but missing the body of the station.

"I don't feel comfortable sending people through the station's force fields until we understand them better. A shuttle could potentially be crushed. We're going to send a fully automated force this first time, at least. It should be able to get what we need without us putting our necks out into that invisible guillotine."

"What machines are we sending, you may ask," Telisa continued. "First, attendants. We'll get five in there and see how long they last."

"What if the attendants are all destroyed?" Arakaki asked.

"Magnus has adapted a stealth sphere to one of his robots. Yat and Marcant are augmenting its software to enable it to open basic Rovan hatches and doors. We hope this will be a long term spy that we can use to gather the information we need."

"Are we just poking around to find living Rovans? Gain Rovan tech?" Barrai asked. "Because I feel like you have a long term objective..."

"You're right," Telisa said. "If there are Rovans, we need to learn to communicate. If not, I want that knowledge base that we lost on the other station. We're going in after it."

"It's a big risk for data that will probably be wiped when we get there," Magnus said.

"We're going to get that data and we're not going to lose anyone doing it," Telisa insisted. "We're going to start hitting some VR scenarios along these lines, and they'll become more realistic as we gain information from S1. That's all for now."

The meeting disbanded.

Yat lingered with Arakaki at the table as the others left.

"What do you think? Live Rovans or no?" Arakaki said.

"No," Yat guessed. "The stations are empty, other than a bunch of those robot bugs of theirs."

Arakaki nodded. "Surely there are some Rovans alive somewhere," she said. "There might have been some in that colony complex that drove us out."

Yat shrugged. "Maybe. But I think their civilization is mostly gone."

"Yat?"

It was Telisa on a private channel.

"Yes?" he responded. He almost added "TM" as he kept hearing Barrai say, but he stopped himself.

"You're not on a sleep shift now, are you?"

"No, I'm ready to help if you need me."

"I don't have a major role for you in this one, I just want you to be watching live and help us breach security. It should be good practice with Rovan systems."

"Sure. I was planning to take in what I could anyway."

"Excellent. We're about to launch the shuttle." She disconnected.

"Who is it?" Arakaki asked.

"Telisa. I have to get to work," Yat said.

"Got it," Arakaki said, rising. "Did Telisa want you FTF for the incursion?"

"No, I'm only monitoring the Rovan security aspects of the probe... but I think I should work alone, away from distractions."

"Such a sweet talker you are," she quipped. Yat knew she would had not taken it wrong. She had made it crystal clear that she appreciated candor and professionalism.

"Good luck," she said. "I'll probably be watching too, on and off."

"See you later."

She left. Yat sat alone in the room.

I suppose this is as good a place as any.

He activated the decor system and turned down the light bars. He set the sound system to play cicadas buzzing on a hot night as a distant thunderstorm approached. Then he focused on the operation in his PV.

Barrai coordinated the approach of the shuttle with the angle of *Sharplight*'s fire position. The shuttle took a station just outside S1's shielding and the *Sharplight*'s targeting computers displayed the planned shot to Yat and anyone else who cared to access it.

Yat was not set up to understand the many layers of data being displayed. His current PV layout was designed to help him keep track of Rovan security systems. He started to tweak his displays and gain familiarity with the new ones.

"Ready to light them up," Barrai said enthusiastically. "Er, or *not* light them up, in this case..."

"Begin," Telisa said.

The tactical displayed a bright line that was the *Sharplight*'s energy strike. It missed the station by a narrow margin. The shuttle accelerated sharply and closed to within thirty meters of the station.

"The shuttle is hard to see," Yat said. As he spoke the shuttle disappeared from view completely, along with the station, leaving a zone of utter blackness.

"The screens are recovering slowly, but at the moment they're blocking out light in a broader spectrum," Barrai said.

"Our contact with the shuttle?"

"Still intact," Barrai reported. "The lower frequencies are less energetic, so less dangerous to them."

Yat switched to a feed coming over from the shuttle. The craft rapidly closed with the station and alighted upon its surface. Within a second or two, the group of attendants darted out to hover within a few centimeters of the hull.

Magnus's robot had its stealth engaged, but it was sending a feed to the shuttle as well. Their machines moved toward the lock they had targeted for the incursion.

"I'm starting work on the airlock," Yat told them.

Marcant and Yat had worked together to create a Rovan incursion suite that included various approaches created by each of them. Yat had to rely upon a method that did not require a physical breach of the station's hull. He started in on the target hatch.

Two of the methods could be attempted in parallel, but the others had to be tried sequentially. He launched the two parallel methods. One completed without success, the other one went longer but had a positive update to offer from its first step. A minute passed.

"It's slower than when you're there in person, looks like," Telisa said neutrally. "Or is there resistance like we encountered at the colony shipyard?"

"No active resistance. Communications are spotty, but I think we have it..."

The airlock opened. Five attendants shot out into a yellow room that looked just like the one the PIT team had entered through on S3. Magnus's spy machine waited for a few seconds, then it followed more slowly.

Yat closed the outer lock. He had not mastered the intricacies of Rovan airlocks versus surface blast doors, but managed to induce a lock cycle. The chamber pressurized and the internal door opened.

The attendants shot off into the station, spiraling wildly. One of the six feeds dropped a second later.

I suppose it was inevitable.

The tactical showed four rovlings lying in wait next to the lock. Five of the attendants made it past them by darting erratically.

The next shot showed an attendant accelerating down a round corridor. Dozens of robots crawled on the interior surface of the corridor at all angles, all surging toward the orb. Despite the crazy spiral course of the attendant, projectiles zeroed in. The feed dropped.

Rovlings. Lots of them.

Yat moved on to another attendant feed. The attendant had made it over a hundred meters into the ship by zipping away every time rovlings threatened it. The orb danced through a field of narrow columns above a series of rectangular vats with robotic arms draped over their openings. The feed went blank, accompanied by a report of overheating.

Laser got it.

The other attendant feeds had dropped as well.

"They're armed and the station is full of them," Arakaki summarized.

"They haven't detected the stealth bot," Telisa said. Yat chose the last remaining feed, being sent to them via the shuttle that dropped the robots off.

Magnus's robot slowly crawled into the Rovan station. Its feed dropped, then picked back up. No rovlings remained in the room adjacent to the lock; Yat supposed if the lock were opened again more of them might come to guard it. The stealthy PIT robot stopped beyond the airlock prep room as rovlings wandered nearby, but they did not react to its presence.

At least this one might survive, Yat thought.

The feed skipped, then it dropped out again.

"No! What got it?" Magnus asked.

"Nothing," Marcant said. "It's still transmitting, but the station's shields are getting stronger, interfering with a dynamic range of frequencies. It's blocking our communications."

"If it blocks radiation coming in, how does the station see out?" Arakaki demanded.

"It doesn't see everything, not all the time," Barrai said. "It probably allows lower, less energetic frequencies through from certain directions at certain times. In other words, it cautiously collects data it needs by peeking out in special ways that the designers believed would be safe."

"The shuttle will keep trying to relay the bot's feed through," Marcant added. "I can see peeps from it here and there, but nothing consistent enough to keep the feed open. We may be able to adjust by using even lower frequencies and sending less data through."

"It's kind of strange that the stations have no external weapons," Yat said. "So many rovlings in there, but other than their protective screens, they're sitting ducks in ship-to-ship combat."

"It is odd, but I assume there was a fleet escort here at one time," Barrai said. "That patrol ship that came by the planet must have been a part of it."

"Only one left? Interesting," Magnus said.

"They may have been drawn away into an engagement elsewhere, or maybe they just gave up," Barrai pointed out. "Who knows?"

The bottom line is: rovlings but no Rovans. Again.

***

"How many rovlings did we find?" Yat asked. The other PIT team members sat around him in a long meeting room. No one had bothered to activate the room's decor, at least not on the shared augmented reality channel; it looked like a clean, gray room with a transparent table, twenty chairs, and six vertical lighting rods.

"The current estimate is twenty thousand," Telisa told them.

Arakaki whistled. "Frag me."

"We've demonstrated we can get shuttles through the screen, and we know the layout over there is almost identical to the empty station we brought back from the brink of destruction. It's time to send a small team over."

"Who?" Arakaki asked. "And why?"

"The way I see it we have two choices," Telisa said. "We can build some specialized machines to try to get the data in the S1 nexus, or we can send two of us."

"Seems obvious to me that the machines should do it," Barrai said. "What's the down side there?"

"The machines won't be as smart as we are. It might be challenging to defeat the security systems at the nexus we found, even Rovan ones, without triggering the erasure of data as we suspect happened to us on S3."

"We have two tries left," Arakaki pointed out.

"Maybe. Or maybe the two active stations communicate. A threat to one may cause the other station to go scorched earth," Marcant said. "But we do have a good chance. As advanced as the Rovans are with the force fields, they're behind in electronic security. We don't even know that much about their technology yet, but we can already hack them eight ways from extinction."

"It might take us the practice from one to get the other right," Magnus said.

"Maybe a hybrid approach would work," Marcant said. "If we can figure out how to communicate through the shields, we could send in machines and back them up remotely."

"Maybe," Telisa said. "Right now, I'm leaning toward sending in the machines. I don't want to lose anyone to the force screens, or the rovling army."

"We must go in ourselves," Maxsym stated.

Yat's eyebrows went up. Telisa and Marcant also looked surprised.

"Maxsym doesn't often give such assertive input, does he?" Yat asked Arakaki privately.

"Seldom," Arakaki replied.

"Why?" Telisa asked Maxsym.

"If these stations are nurseries as we suspect, then think about what that means the data is. It was there to educate the young Rovans. It would tell us all about them; their values, history, sciences, and technologies. It would be ridiculously valuable to us."

Everyone sat in silence for a moment, working his assertions over.

"Then you want us to send TMs to ensure that we end up in possession of this data?" Magnus asked.

"Yes. Like the tissue samples, this is so important the risk is worth it."

"If we did send people, who would they be?" asked Barrai.

"The best TMs for the job would be Yat and Adair," Telisa answered.

"Yat and Adair? I was sure... it would be someone else," Marcant said.

"It's tempting to go myself, but I have to consider everyone's talents and... I may be taking more of an oversight role going forward," Telisa said.

Telisa sounded reluctant to mention it. But most of Yat's attention was on himself at the moment. He might be going in!

"Yat's smooth with the Rovan physical security and he has the creativity to overcome unexpected roadblocks. Adair is our best bet to copy the data quickly and cleanly."

"I think I'll be wanting that force field pack now," Adair said.

"You would both have force field packs and stealth spheres," Telisa said. "You would activate the force fields before your shuttle goes through the screens. If the shuttle is damaged or destroyed by the Rovan shields when we slip you in, those packs might save your lives."

"But then they'd be trapped inside," Marcant said.

"If things go that badly, we'll fire on the station, do whatever it takes to get you back out," Telisa promised.

"Let's get ready," Yat said.

"No. Sleep first," Telisa ordered. "Magnus and Marcant will think about what equipment and software is necessary and prepare it."

***

Telisa looked at Yat at the shuttle ramp.

"Good luck," Telisa said.

She seems hesitant. Maybe she doesn't think I can handle it.

"Thanks."

Telisa looked over her shoulder down the bay, then back at Yat.

"If it goes south, I'll hop in another shuttle and come in after you myself, if I have to. We have your back."

"Got it," he said confidently. He realized Telisa really was concerned.

This is hard for her. Sending me out on a mission and not coming along herself.

Telisa walked back out. Adair was folded up in the back of the shuttle.

"Ready to do this, jelly-brain?" it asked.

"Yes."

"Good, because if we fail it'll make me look bad."

Yat smiled. He flopped down in the pilot seat, though it did not matter much—the shuttle flew itself and took orders from any authorized link.

Yat activated the shuttle's stealth systems and let it ease out of the bay. Yat was struck by the size of the *Sharplight*—sometimes he forgot—and yet it was small compared to the Rovan stations. Two other shuttles had left with them, holding robots that would breach other spots on the station to distract the rovlings from Adair and Yat.

"I've got control of your shuttle," Barrai said to Yat. "The power rings I need are charged," she continued on the PIT channel. "Ready to coordinate."

"Adair and Yat, activate your Rovan packs," Telisa ordered.

"On," Adair said.

Yat turned activated his force field.

"Force field on," Yat replied.

Yat watched as *Sharplight* computers took direct control of the shuttle. The shuttle rotated away from its heading vector. He received a warning of imminent acceleration.

"Configured for penetration... I always wanted to say that," Barrai said.

"Go," Telisa ordered.

"Firing," Barrai said.

Yat grunted as his seat pressed into his back. The shuttle shook hard.

"If you can hear me, we're through," Yat said.

"Copy that. Be fast," Telisa said.

The shuttle closed with the station until it hovered a meter away.

"We're on," Yat said to Adair. He nodded and unstrapped from the pilot's seat.

"Wait," Adair said. "We have to make sure all the distractions made it through and are in place. Otherwise this'll be an FTF between us and twenty thousand angry rovlings."

"I see your point," Yat said.

Yat took out his specialized weapon. It was a one-off design that Magnus had produced, with four small barrels above a Rovan helix launcher.

Yat did not stand. It might be a few minutes until the other shuttles had entered the station and distracted the rovlings. He took a deep breath and let it out slowly.

"I hate this part," Yat said aloud. "The worst part is always the waiting."

"You think it's bad for you? For an AI, a few minutes is like a hundred years of your time," Adair said.

"No way. Really?"

"Nah. I'm just screwing with you," Adair said brightly.

Yat smiled.

The shuttle vibrated slightly as it dropped a breacher onto the Rovan station. The breacher would cut through the station's hull and create a temporary airlock, allowing Yat and Adair to enter closer to the computer nexus. The team also hoped that by not using a Rovan airlock, their entrance might go undetected for longer.

"They're going in now," Adair said. "I say we go in... twenty seconds."

"Right behind you," Yat said.

Yat heard a whine from the breacher as it cut into the station's hull.

"Let's get in there," Adair said. The shuttle door released.

Adair hurtled through the opening like a penguin diving into a hole in the ice. Yat followed, clambering through feet first. When he dropped into the corridor, he saw only the sealed portal before him. He turned back, searching for Adair. He found his teammate clinging to the yellow and gray ceiling.

"Go go," Adair urged.

Yat nodded. He knelt before the door and sent two attendants forward to scan the perimeter.

Just like the one in S3.

Yat had studied the configuration in that station, looking for ways to make a stealthier entrance. This time, Yat tried to isolate the door from the nexus behind it. He did not want it to tell any other systems it had opened.

101

As he started work, he was aware of time pressure, but then he fell into his plan, trying option after option, completing step after step.

"I believe it's isolated. First attempt starting now... "

Yat took a deep breath and kept at it.

"Second attempt... third attempt..."

The door opened.

"My turn!" Adair said enthusiastically. The AI sounded like it was all a game.

"I have your back," Yat said, turning his back on the door to cover the corridor of their breach point. "Not that you have a back."

"Sure I do," Adair transmitted from within, feigning hurt.

"Concentrate on the mission," Yat urged.

"I assure you I am. I can easily converse with a jelly-brain or two at the same time without—"

Adair stopped talking. Yat assumed it was for the best. He sent one of his four attendants out past the entrance hole to hold station at the first pair of red stripes in the corridor. Yat could see the far side about thirty meters distant. Six rovling tubes emptied into the corridor between his position and the end. Yat sent two grenades rolling down the corridor. They dodged into rovling tubes to wait.

His tactical only showed himself and Adair, but his link got a report that the other invaders were heavily engaged and would not last long.

Yat took cover behind a pipe or support beam on his right. Then he crouched. After a moment he shifted nervously, opening up some space on his right between his Veer suit and the wall, thinking that if he had to activate his Rovan pack, the field might damage something, or even snap him away forcefully, injuring him.

"How long—"

"Progress is being made," Adair said brightly.

The tactical sent Yat a warning that rovlings headed toward him.

"They'll get here before I'm done," Adair said.

"I've got it," Yat told Adair. "Just finish!"

Yat activated his shield, pointed his weapon down the corridor, and waited.

The seconds ticked by. Yat heard noises filtering in from the rovling tubes nearby. Two rovlings approached from down the corridor.

Yat held his fire. He did not want to waste any of his ammunition. The rovlings sent projectiles his way, but they bounced off his shield. When two more rovlings scuttled out, he activated the weapon.

Whoosh. Bang!

Four tiny missiles launched and swerved toward the rovlings. Less than a second later, the four alien machines shattered, sending debris flying away from Yat. The reprieve was brief. A second later more rovlings scampered out over the shattered remains of their brethren. Two, three... five. Already more projectiles were ricocheting off his shield.

Whoosh. Bang!

Yat shot again, obliterating more rovlings. Some smoke rose from the debris and rapidly moved toward him.

Air flowing this way... from an army of them coming.

Yat set the helix launcher to fire twice, then switched back to his missiles. He hoped the glue might slow the first ones and block the rest for a few more seconds.

"Adair..."

Ka-Blam!

One of his grenades exploded in a tube. More debris flew out into the corridor.

Rovlings charged out of other tubes at the same time a stream of them turned the corner at the end of the corridor. Yat fired his two helices at the front group.

Smack. Smack. Thwap!

Several rovlings were bound together, scrabbling, but more came across the ceiling to get around them. Yat fired again, sending four tiny missiles out to shatter more rovlings.

Whoosh. Bang!

"*Adair...*"

"I have it," Adair said. "Let's scat."

"I hope that means run, because I'm already running," Yat said. He leaped straight up toward the forced breach cover and told his last grenade to detach and cover the choke point. Adair met him mid-flight, adding additional thrust through Yat's feet.

"Yapzers!" Yat exclaimed as he hurtled toward the shuttle connection at least twice as fast as he had anticipated. He put his arms forward and dove upward into the shuttle. He struck the roof of the cargo area and tumbled away out of control.

Ka-Blam! Ka-Blam!

Adair had more limbs and attendants. The Terran AI managed to swing in and close the incursion hatch swiftly and cleanly. Two seconds later, Yat felt the shuttle shift as they detached.

"Underway!" Adair said cheerily. "Keep your force field on!"

Yat muscled his way into the nearest seat and strapped himself in. His screen kept him from directly contacting the seat. Adrenaline still coursed through his system. He tried to catch his breath and regain his wits.

"Coordinate with me, I'll cut you—" Barrai said, but the transmission cut off.

"Problem," Adair said.

"Yes?" Yat responded. He had not had time to switch from battle mode into thinking like a shuttle pilot.

"This will be hard to time unless we can coordinate with Barrai through the—"

"What?"

The shuttle kicked to the side sharply. Yat's seat rotated to lock him in place against the acceleration, though he felt a wrenching in his upper spine.

"Still in one piece, jelly-brain?" Adair asked.

"Ugh," Yat replied unintelligibly.

"Are you all right? Did you get the data?" demanded Telisa.

"We have it," Adair reported. "And a lot of data it is."

"That's a huge amount of information... enough to, say, educate young Rovans!" Marcant said. Yat assumed that Marcant was already checking out their prize.

"Though that fits well with our favored theory of this place's function, it's also possible that this whole station is a kind of... backup of their civilization," Maxsym said.

"It's a win. Thank you, TMs," Telisa said.

Yat just breathed and waited for adrenaline's grip to release itself.

Chapter 11

Maxsym worked late into his normal sleep shift. Because of the possibility of more Rovan patrol ships appearing, he had temporarily transferred to the *Sharplight*. He holed up in his secondary quarters and established connections to his normal work resources on the *Iridar*.

The first priority was to analyze the Rovan tissue and learn more about their basic biology. He faithfully mapped the tissues and kicked off the simulations of their growth and processes on the *Iridar*, however, something else would not stop bothering him.

Where were the Rovans? Why were the stations not making more of them?

The team had learned about the layout of S3; they had left an attendant and a soldier bot behind on the station to find their way into every nook and cranny. Maxsym considered the data useful only in that it told them about the other stations; it was pretty clear that something had gone wrong with S3 and that could also be why it was not a functioning nursery.

S1 and S2 seemed to have working spinners and plentiful power, a capable rovling workforce, and an operational control nexus. Had production been shut down when the Rovans left? Or had the resources been depleted?

Maxsym could not know the answer to the first question, so he focused on gathering evidence for the second. He started with S3. It had many storage spaces and liquid holding tanks. Maxsym had the robots check the materials stored. The soldier robot had lesser sensors than the Vovokan attendant, so most of the hustle had to come from the attendant. Maxsym found that over thirty percent of the containers and tanks were empty. Another forty percent were in their last twenty percent of capacity.

So the evidence is that S3 is severely depleted.

That supported the idea that they had run out of what they needed to produce another generation of Rovans. However, there was another branch to consider there: perhaps S3 had been drained of resources when its spinner started to go bad. Perhaps S1 and S2 had onloaded those resources before S3 left the stable zone.

Maxsym opened a connection to Magnus.

"Magnus?"

"Here," Magnus responded in a few seconds.

"I'd like to reroute our spy to this room," Maxsym said, providing a path to the nearest group of storage tanks.

"Sure," Magnus said. "What are you looking for?"

"I have reason to believe the stations may be running out of certain resources. I'd like to confirm what I've found on S3 here on S1 to rule out the possibility that they drained S3 when it began to drift."

"Ah, interesting. The bot is on its way, but we're taking it slow. It should arrive in about an hour."

"Thank you," Maxsym said and told the channel he had nothing more to send. The connection dropped.

Maxsym anticipated that the other station would also show signs of depletion, so he continued that train of thought. Did the supplies come from the station on the rocky planet? Were the stations depleted because of the death of the Rovan there?

Doubtful. That place provided water and minerals, likely supplies useful for constructing the stations in the first place.

He watched the machines start to make sense of Rovan biology while he waited for the spy to confirm his suspicions. The cells suggested that Rovans mated in pairs like Terrans, but an anomaly emerged: there were two very different types of cells. Maxsym's first guess was that one type was for Rovans and the other for rovlings, but that idea fizzled quickly when neither group of cells matched tissue he had sampled from the wild rovlings on the colony planet.

Maxsym was thoroughly mystified by the time their spy machine had arrived at the desired location. He forced himself away from the cell analyses in progress and told the machine to make a round of measurements.

The containers on S1 showed severe depletion. That would have made him happy a few minutes ago, but now he was already embroiled in the next mystery.

Maxsym watched the simulated progressions as the cell masses grew. It was slow going and there was a huge number of branches to the work, because the cells in the simulations often died out since the machines did not know what to provide from the outside to enable their proper growth and survival. It was more than simply simulating food supplies; many other chemicals would be needed, for example Rovan hormone analogues.

Some of the more successful branches started to produce tissues Maxsym could recognize... Rovan shells. The other masses were producing things that looked more as Maxsym would expect: the Rovans themselves. He shook his head.

The crazy roundabout ways that nature gets things done...

After another hour, Maxsym found his eyes closing against his will. He decided to make his report. He could easily send Telisa a pointer to his data and conclusions, but he knew she preferred they speak about it so that she could ask questions.

"I have a report to make," Maxsym sent her.

"I assume it's about the cell samples we were able to obtain," she replied.

"Well, no, I have discovered... more questions than answers there."

"Tell me."

"There are two types of cells. Both seem to be viable tissue. I think one is... for the shell. The other, for the rest of the organism. But these types are so different, it's as if they come from two different organisms. Neither match the wild rovlings we found on the dead colony."

"Their shells are... other living things! Another amazing symbiosis?"

"A solid hypothesis. It appears to be a symbiosis so advanced neither type can live long without the other. If we go back far enough, perhaps that was the original cause of this oddity. Rovans may have required sex *twice* to procreate. Once for the Rovan proper, which I suppose may have gestated for a time, then again later to combine genetic material for the shell."

"I wonder if the baby is viable if the shell father differs from the... previous father."

"Great minds think alike. I'm working on that now. It's entirely possible that some of the genetic material is saved aside for later, as some Earth creatures can do."

"You said you had more questions than answers, but it sounds like progress."

"Well, everything I told you is a guess. Another guess would be that..."

"Yes?"

"Perhaps two Rovans mated once. This then produced a young Rovan with no shell. Then the *offspring* may have mated with another Rovan to combine the genetic material for its shell."

"By the Five! That is... quite alien."

"Indeed."

"Okay, what was your intended report about then?"

"I was going to tell you that I studied the materials used by these stations to operate."

"Okay..."

Maxsym shared a pointer to the map of S3 he had started with.

"These areas here are tanks and bins. They supply raw materials. By sampling these, we can probably tell what is needed."

"You say, 'what is needed'. I assume that means, it's no longer stored there?"

"Stations S1 and S3 are depleted," Maxsym said. "They simply ran out of supplies. I think this is why the stations are shut down."

"One less mystery in our pile. Thank you for your work."

"I'm depleted as well," Maxsym said. "I'm headed to sleep."

"Okay, go recharge, Maxsym," she said. "We'll brainstorm next steps soon."

***

Maxsym woke with a mind filled with thoughts of Rovans. He had not taken enough sleep, but the shift was over and he wanted to find out what the plan for the stations would be.

The station we saved is probably too broken. The young would need rovling caretakers anyway. But the rovlings will be in our way on the other two stations.

Maxsym dressed rapidly. The ship told him that Telisa, Magnus, Arakaki and Marcant were in the mess hall. Maxsym hurried out of his quarters and stomped down the corridor to join them.

"It's possible that all new Rovans were made on stations like these," Telisa was saying.

"I could see it, but it makes me wonder what kind of society they had," Yat said. "Growing all the young together in such controlled environments means they would be able to indoctrinate entire generations in a uniform way. A kind of monolithic empire setup."

"It could have been a cult," Arakaki said. "I've heard stories from the frontier. Whole groups leave the Core Worlds to establish 'utopias' and fill them with programmed children."

"Maybe that data will tell us," Telisa said. Predictably, she looked toward Marcant.

"You know we'll work on it," he said.

"This is an amazing find. We'll take all the samples we need, copy the data over, and go on our way," Telisa said.

"What? I assumed we would do the obvious," Maxsym blurted. He sounded more alarmed than he meant to.

"The obvious... what's that?" Telisa asked.

Is this a joke?

"As I explained, these stations are starved of certain material resources, but they still have the source tissue. We should resupply them. They may then manufacture more Rovans!" Maxsym concluded grandly. "We could study them, talk to them, tell them what we've discovered of their race and let them be our guides."

"A bunch of juvenile Rovans? I don't think that would work," Magnus said.

"Why not? Remember, these would be *fully educated* Rovans. If we can't find what happened to the original Rovans, this is the next best thing."

Telisa still looked stunned, though he could see her mulling over the possibilities. Magnus and Arakaki did not look happy. Maxsym slowly realized 'the obvious' might be a tough sell.

I'm actually going to have to convince them...

"Don't worry, we're going to do it," Marcant sent him privately. Maxsym looked over at Marcant. Marcant winked at him.

Michael McCloskey

Chapter 12

The PIT team gathered in a mess hall. For the first time, Telisa saw real tension between the team members. With Imanol, there had been a few localized pressures, but now the entire team sat in tense, antagonistic poses.

It's up to me to hold them together.

Telisa doubted herself; she had not had to do this before.

"I think we all know what needs to be discussed, but Maxsym, why don't you start by reiterating what you'd like to do with these stations," she opened.

Maxsym stood eagerly.

"If we supply these centers with more materials, then I believe that they will start manufacturing Rovans," Maxsym said. "Marcant and Yat have identified huge amounts of stored data which we believe is used to educate the young Rovans. These stations are essentially Rovan factories... or nurseries, if you prefer."

Maxsym paused.

"It is my belief that the Rovans created these stations specifically to ensure that their race could be rebuilt in case of disaster. Such a disaster has obviously befallen them. We're their rescuers. We can give them another chance. With our help, perhaps the Rovans can now succeed where they could not before. It would not be unlike when we helped the Celarans."

Maxsym sat back down.

Arakaki saw a chance to respond and took it. "These centers will warm up a bunch of Rovan embryos, birth them... *raise* them, and then what? We can't unilaterally do that. If you cause creatures to come into the world, you're responsible for them. We don't even know *how* to be responsible for a bunch of aliens. It would likely be an affront to their ancestors to raise them like Terrans. The Rovans must have their own cultural standards and practices."

"Well, technically, the Rovans made these stations for this purpose, and it was them who set this up. All we would do is supply the resources that they need to fulfill their purpose," Maxsym said. "Then *they* would bring more Rovans into existence."

"Just because an alien race made something doesn't mean you understand why they did it and under what circumstances it was supposed to be used," Yat said. "We're meddling with their very lives."

"Marcant? Did you want to speak?" Telisa prompted.

Marcant took a second to compose himself.

"If the Rovans created by these stations were helpless young, I would be against doing this lightly. In that case, I would advise perhaps a decade of study before attempting it. But these will be more than mindless children," Marcant said. "These stations have vast repositories of knowledge and thousands of rovling attendants. That must be to care for and teach the young. Most likely they have methods of imparting knowledge way beyond what we have. These 'children' would mature to be more advanced than the average Terran, albeit rather ill-equipped to tackle the universe since they would lack a material civilization of their own."

Barrai stood and took her turn.

"There are too many unknowns. You're making too many assumptions. First, you don't know if that knowledge is for education. You don't know what will happen until you flip some switch that can't be unflipped. Secondly, we don't know what happened to the Rovans. We should know what happened to them before we make more. Finally, what if the Rovans turn out to be a horrible, despicable species that were wiped out for a reason? What if Rovans make Vovokans look like playful puppies?"

Adair stepped up on its robotic legs and took a turn to speak.

"It's true we don't know for sure if the knowledge is strictly to educate young Rovans. It may be that it was a repository of the knowledge of their race, hidden here to preserve it. However, that knowledge may contain answers to some of the uncertainties previously mentioned: maybe it describes what was happening to the Rovans. Maybe it contains the key to solving whatever issue it was they faced. Maybe it is us who will next be threatened by whatever wiped them out. This could be our fastest way to learn about the danger."

"As to the doubts expressed about the Rovans themselves: The knowledge repository probably contains Rovan histories which could tell us what kind of race they are. I don't know how long it will take us to understand them. Perhaps years. I also don't know if it's our place to decide whether they deserve to live again based upon our judgements."

Adair continued.

"Let's consider the case you bring up: suppose the Rovans are aggressive. Dangerous. One safe way to find out would be to study a small group of them in a restricted environment like right here. We would be forewarned before anything *really* bad could happen."

"Are we going to deny a race life because of a bunch of unanswered questions?" Adair asked. "We made the decision to let our enemy, the Quarus, go on existing. Surely the Rovans deserve the same chance. They could go and live on the Rovan colony world, complete with all those supplies."

Yat replied.

"We can't unleash a bunch of aliens onto that world without knowing why the Rovans died off in the first place," Yat said. "We could be sending them to their deaths."

"I agree that we could certainly try to learn more before proceeding, but in the end, if we make no major discoveries that contraindicate action, I would go ahead with it," Adair said.

Marcant could not contain himself.

"Imagine if Terrans were wiped out. If some aliens found a bunch of Terran zygotes, wouldn't we want them to bring us back?" he exclaimed.

"So we could live as experiments? Curiosities?" Arakaki asked.

"Or so they could be used by some alien cult with totally unknown cultural dispositions?" Yat added.

"Can you stop forgetting that these Rovans will be fully educated in their own values and culture," Marcant growled.

"We haven't forgotten your *theory* that will happen. Have you forgotten how old these stations likely are?" Yat asked. "What if something goes wrong? There are no Rovans here to fix it. What if the young are kept alive but their education systems fail?"

Their voices were rising. Telisa did not want to dampen the discussion, but she did want it to cool down somewhat. She decided Magnus would offer a measured opinion.

"Magnus?"

Magnus spoke without standing up.

"This decision could affect all Terrans. I'm not sure the PIT team can speak for our entire race. The Celarans should also be consulted," he said. "Perhaps they have a view on this that would surprise us."

"But we can't pass the decision off to our government," Telisa said. "That's tantamount to just asking Shiny. As Team Members, we're actually powerful enough to make decisions like this, if you believe he's our rightful leader."

"I think we should consult the Celarans for their opinion, and we should search for living Rovans for longer before trying to become their keepers," Magnus summarized. Barrai and Yat nodded. Arakaki looked angrily at Marcant.

Magnus stopped and it was apparent he had no more conditions to add.

"So unless I've seriously misunderstood anyone, those in favor of reviving the Rovans are Maxsym, Marcant... and myself. Those opposed are Arakaki, Yat, and Barrai. Magnus and Adair have given certain preconditions."

Marcant rose to his feet. "The majority ultimately want to revive the Rovans, though possibly not today."

Arakaki and Barrai opened their mouths to reply.

"Stop," Telisa said. "We need to separate, cool down, and think. I won't be making any hasty orders. This is a big step and clearly we aren't ready to take it. I know I call the shots on most of our operations, but this is bigger than all of us. I'm not ready to drag PIT members in on reviving a dead race unless we have a stronger consensus."

Marcant grimaced as if someone was digging into a wound in his flesh. Maxsym's face was slack in dismay.

These people are all amazingly smart and talented. Passionate. This is a byproduct of that. It's what I get when I stymie them.

Telisa watched everyone filter out and wondered what to do.

"Magnus, if you would stay," she sent privately. He returned to a seat across from her.

After the others left, he looked at her expectantly.

"I hope you're not going to—"

"Lean on you? No," she said. "If we go to Blackhab and fill in the Celarans, do you think we should involve our new team of scientists?"

Magnus rubbed his chin and stared off into space for a moment.

"Well, in one regard, they're simply Terran citizens like us. They aren't part of the government, though some used to have ties to the Space Force."

"The way I see it, telling them has advantages and drawbacks. On the good side, they are alien experts."

"Alien tech experts," Magnus said.

"They're intelligent. And though they study alien tech now they have backgrounds in xenoarchaeology and xenobiology as well as xenocybernetics."

Magnus nodded.

"On the down side," Telisa continued, "being scientists, they would be tempted to say yes to a revivification program in order to satisfy their personal curiosity and advance our own scientific aims."

"Like Marcant and Maxsym," Magnus prompted.

Tactful of him to leave me off that list.

"Maybe."

"Here's another angle," Magnus said. "The PIT team is hardly a representative sample of Terran civilization. If we're only half and half on the issue, then the average Terran might be against it."

Telisa smiled.

"Honestly I think the average Core Worlder would say do it just for the hell of it, and hope the Rovans have some good VRs to enjoy."

Magnus nodded. "Your comments about Shiny being in charge were not lost on me, either. We have no genuine government to defer the decision to. The Space Force and CWS are hardly replacements."

Telisa nodded.

"Well, keep thinking on it. We'll have to do something eventually."

"Will we? We could do nothing."

"If we don't do it, and we handed it all over to Shiny, who knows what he'd do?" Telisa said.

"Don't tell him about it," Magnus replied.

Telisa nodded again. "I don't think I will."

Michael McCloskey

Chapter 13

Magnus worked over an attendant in a fabrication shop on the *Sharplight*. His hobby on the voyage had been devising ways of dealing with rovlings, and he had returned to that pastime while the team depressurized for a few shifts. Magnus had several modified attendants set out before him. His current set of experiments involved hardening attendants so they could damage rovlings through collision. Magnus had decided hurting the rovlings' bodies was not feasible without killing the attendant immediately, but he pursued another line of ideas that focused on damaging the rovlings' weapons, sensors, or legs.

At some point, his link made him aware that Adair had arrived in the shop. Magnus looked up with one of his prototypes in his hands.

"What's this?" Adair asked.

"Legbreaker," Magnus announced. He smiled.

"Excuse me?"

"Well, you see this crescent of material I've added? It adds considerable structural integrity with minimal weight increase. The attendant darts in at a rovling, and this crescent breaks its leg."

"Ah. An anti-rovling weapon," Adair said.

"Exactly!"

"Won't they just shoot it with an energy beam?" Adair asked.

Magnus sighed.

"Most of the rovlings we've faced had projectile weapons," he said. "Still, if you have suggestions to make it better, tell me."

"I think your other robots are better equipped to deal with the rovlings," Adair said. "The problem is that the Rovans are generally more advanced than we are, combined with the fact that they've been using rovlings for warfare since their ancient times. The attendants are fast and sophisticated, but their mission is very different."

"My reasoning is that we have attendants with us anyway, so they may as well be equipped to help fight rovlings."

"We sure do a lot of preparation to fight rovlings when all we want to do is make friends with the Rovans," Adair said.

"Yeah, that's too bad," Magnus agreed. "But we have to live to the point where we find them and make peace with their little watchdogs."

Magnus looked at the prototype in his hands and frowned.

"So as you say... they're more advanced, and had a lot of experience with this," he said. "What recourse do we have? Wait until we advance to the point where we know more than they did?"

"Hit 'em where they're weak," Adair said. "We already know the Rovans had poor electronic security."

"So we should be hacking the rovlings, not fighting them physically," Magnus concluded.

"I think so, yes."

A task which would be better suited to Marcant.

Magnus had not heard or seen much of Maxsym and Marcant. He suspected they were using the time to hone their arguments, or just prepare for what they saw as an inevitable step to revive the Rovans.

"We need your help with that," Magnus said. "Can you start a new project?"

"Sure!" Adair replied enthusiastically. The AI liked to be a needed member of the team like most everyone else.

Magnus decided to stop thinking about attendants and burn some energy.

"Thanks. I'm taking a break," he told Adair.

He left the shop and started to run. He tried to leave his mind idle for a while, but he inevitably ended up wondering what would happen with the recent team split.

Yat and Arakaki were keeping to themselves. They had spent a lot of time together since becoming a couple, now they were even more isolated.

I wonder what she sees in him? He is an adventurer of sorts, but I had her pegged for one who liked military types.

Magnus supposed that after the loss of her true love, she had decided to try a different type of person.

Good for her.

A meeting appeared on the PIT team's schedule, two hours in the future. Magnus headed in to get cleaned up and participate.

***

"Has anyone changed their position on the Rovan nursery issue since we last discussed it?"

Telisa's question got no response from those gathered on the bridge of the *Sharplight*. Everyone was present— and calm. Magnus felt they would accept Telisa's decision, whatever it was going to be.

Telisa wasted no time getting down to it.

125

"As the leader I have to make a decision. Nevertheless, I don't want to proceed hastily, and I don't want to rip our team apart over this. So this is what we'll do: Arakaki, Yat, Magnus and Adair are going to take the *Iridar* ahead to the next Rovan colony location. Your mission will be to see if there are any Rovan survivors we can contact. That would have many benefits if they turn out to be peaceful, and they might be very happy to learn about these nurseries."

That caught Magnus off guard. He saw surprised looks from the others as well.

"With due respect, Team Member, I'd like to go with them," Barrai said.

"No, I need you to stick with the *Sharplight*, as you're critical to this ship's operation and well being. Don't worry, if the others find Rovans, then we'll be consulting with them about the stations."

"Then perhaps we could go in the *Sharplight*," Arakaki said.

"No, because the rest of us are going to get supplies for these stations," Telisa said. "The *Iridar* is too small to carry a significant amount of resources to bring here. You'll be able to use the smaller, stealthier ship to look for Rovans. You don't need to make contact with them, just find out if any are still alive."

"Then what?" Magnus asked.

"We meet back here. If you haven't found Rovans at the next colony site, we'll go check another. We can also collect the thoughts of the Celarans. They will have their own perspective, and Lee was going to check out another possible colony site. Hopefully what we learn will help to unify the team on this."

126

Magnus mulled over Telisa's decision. On the one hand, she was being very reasonable to hold off until they learned more. And she avoided the animosity of making a decision half the team was set against, at least in the short term. On the other hand, was she showing a lack of will for strong leadership? Most leaders eventually had to make unpopular decisions and stick to them.

Magnus decided he liked this way more than how it had been in the Space Force where he followed orders he did not like and no one wanted to hear his opinion.

Marcant and Adair left without comment. Telisa hesitated, then left as well. Barrai did not look like she was going anywhere else anyway. She probably often worked from this bridge.

Arakaki walked over to Magnus and dispelled his thoughts.

"How long you need? We may as well head over to *Iridar* together."

"An hour," Magnus said. Arakaki nodded. Expediency suited her.

"We'll meet you in an hour," she said.

"An hour?" Maxsym said. "I'll need at least two to shut things down over there and get what I need over to the *Sharplight*."

Maxsym was making the opposite move—from *Iridar* to *Sharplight*. Maxsym did not look happy.

"You'll be back in your Vovokan labs soon," Magnus assured him.

"Yes. It's regrettable we can't take *Iridar* and leave you with Barrai. This means my research into the Rovan physiology will take longer," he said. "But Telisa's reasoning was sound. The *Sharplight* can carry much more and the *Iridar* is stealthier."

"Please get over there and start packing," Arakaki told him. "I'm eager to get started."

Magnus smiled. Arakaki was trying hard to be respectful while pushing Maxsym into hurrying. Maxsym nodded and strode out for the shuttle bay.

Magnus smiled at her.

You know damn well he's going to take a long time to get out of there.

Arakaki sighed. She knew what he was thinking.

"Maybe we'll be underway by tomorrow," she said grimly.

Magnus left the bridge for his quarters. He was calculating what he needed. In an hour he could move several sets of gear over to the shuttle.

As Magnus packed his few possessions, Telisa came into his quarters.

"I'll miss you," she said. She suddenly threw her arms around him and caught him in her iron grip.

"For once, I'm actually glad I didn't completely agree with you," Magnus said.

"Oh? Have you decided to join the nays?"

"No, I mean I think this is a good plan. Those with reservations can go search for Rovans and take an active part in making things play out their way. If there are still living Rovans out there, we don't want to go ahead without their involvement."

"That's the plan. We won't go ahead until we have buy in from Rovans, or believe they're extinct."

"If we don't find any... not sure we'll think they're extinct for sure. We may be back to where we started. Though I wonder what the Celarans will say."

"Once we've searched all the known Rovan sites, it will be a subtly different position to argue from," Telisa said. "We'll cross that bridge when we come to it."

Magnus nodded and lugged his gear out.

Michael McCloskey

Chapter 14

Arakaki took one look at the *Iridar*'s status in her PV and could tell something was very wrong. She accessed the team channel and sent a high priority message.

"We have a situation here," she said. The channel only had four TMs on it: Magnus, Yat, Adair, and herself. They were only a week out from the binary system, headed toward the next suspected Rovan colony.

"I'm here," Magnus said. "I'm just looking over... oh damn."

"Yeah," she said.

"What is it?" Yat asked. He sounded tired. It was not surprising, since they had staggered their sleep shifts on the voyage. Yat had likely been asleep.

"We're moving at sublight speed, and I have absolutely no idea where we are," Arakaki said. "There aren't any stars nearby."

"There are other ships out there!" Adair reported.

"I'm activating our stealth systems," Magnus said.

"I'll change course," Arakaki said. She did not relish the idea of a space battle in an unfamiliar ship without the *Sharplight* to back them up.

We're deep in interstellar space.

Arakaki asked the ship why it had brought down the spinner. The ship responded with a complex PV pane showing the entire propulsion system in three dimensions along with various components in red together with their error diagnostics. None of the displayed results were straightforward.

"Something's wrong with the spinner," she said. "Maybe more than one something."

"I'm on it," Adair said.

"You can bet that's no coincidence," Magnus said. "It didn't just happen to dump us out here by all these other ships for no reason."

"So even if we want to leave, we can't," Yat summarized.

"Not now, but the ship says it's trying to fix the problem," Adair said.

"Let's see who's out here with us," Magnus said.

"I don't recognize any of them yet. Neither does the *Iridar*," Arakaki said.

"Guys! Take a look at this one," Yat said.

Arakaki checked his pointer. She saw a huge object among the debris. It was as large as a Vovokan battleship.

"We don't know that hull shape... an absorption pattern might help. but I can't launch active scans with our stealth on," Arakaki said.

"We could launch a probe. But I'd rather not announce our presence," Magnus said.

"Agreed."

"It looks Rovan," Yat said.

"A Rovan ship," Arakaki echoed. "It must have been stopped here same as us?"

"A lot of these other ships look decidedly un-Rovan," Magnus said.

"It was attacked by all these others? It must have put up a hell of a fight. Most of them have been ruptured," Arakaki noted.

"At this point who knows who attacked who?" Yat said. "Maybe this is the enemy that killed the Rovans off."

Of course. He's right. If they had spacefaring enemies...

"This is interstellar space," Magnus said. "How did we happen to come by this place?"

"You said it yourself. It's no coincidence," Yat pointed out.

"I mean, was our course changed? How did our course happen to intersect all this... unless these ships are here because they're on the line between the same two stars."

"We're on course. It's like a blockade in the void between two stars," Adair said.

"Doesn't the line move over time with the drift of these stars?" Yat asked.

"Yes. They may be moving to stay between them as the stars move relative to each other," Adair said. "Also, it can't be a very tight line. It must somehow affect a very wide cylinder of space between the two systems."

"Well all the ships are within a few light seconds of each other out here," Yat said. "There are five clusters of them."

"We came to find out if there are any living Rovans. Well, here's a gigantic Rovan ship. We should try to contact it," Arakaki said.

"It obliterated all these ships. Let's learn more first," Magnus said.

Arakaki looked at Yat. He shrugged.

"Adair?" she asked.

"I vote for staying hidden!" Adair said. "We can come back with the *Sharplight*... and maybe a few more ships... or a battle group..."

"Fine. Let's get closer to one of the other alien ships then," Arakaki said.

"I want to, but can that give us away?" Yat asked.

"Yes. Yes it can," Adair said.

"But don't you want to know who the Rovans were fighting out here in the vastness of space?" Arakaki asked.

Yat answered for Adair. "Yes, but I also want to know what's so special about this place. Is it a blockade or is there something worth fighting over out here? How are ships' spinners brought down like that?"

"These other ships are long dead," Magnus said. "We can go in slowly and get some pretty good information on them. It'll be a lot safer than knocking on the doors of that huge Rovan ship."

Magnus brought the *Iridar* around. He selected a cluster of the alien ships and edged their ship closer. Their passive sensors took in what they could.

Arakaki saw a ship that had been sheared in half. It was long and slender, with a cross section shaped like a flattened hexagon. The center was hollow, but the interior volume limited, as the hull was extremely thick, easily ten times thicker than a Terran or Celaran hull.

"The exposed interiors are confusing me," Yat said. "There aren't decks like our ships. These are hollow inside like Celaran ships, but the space is a lot smaller and more intricate."

"The patterns are complicated. It's almost fractal," Arakaki said. "Maybe these critters were small. Like mouse-sized."

"I'm thinking these were automated ships," Magnus said. "Maybe the Rovans were fighting some kind of artificial superintelligence."

"Then it's a good thing I'm here," Adair said brightly.

Adair was joking. Arakaki knew that although Adair was brighter than almost any Terran, it fell short of most standards for the term 'superintelligence'. The problem of diminishing returns in intelligence made such a thing impossible—at least for now.

"I can see their weapons," Adair said. It sent along a pointer. "These bulbs are common across the ships. They used them to project energy."

"No signs of projectiles or missiles?" Magnus asked.

"Not that I can recognize. But it's still possible," Adair said.

Arakaki found a chunk of a ship floating amid the local pack of defeated vessels. It looked to be a piece of thick hull. The inside was mottled and filled with narrow passages and crevices. She thought over more possibilities.

"There could also have been one big, very weird thing living in there that couldn't move around much," Arakaki said. "If the ships were automated, why would there be that weird space inside?"

"Any number of possible reasons," Adair said. "Internal spaces could have been used to allow for internal repairs by small machines, or for keeping the ship's mass lower while providing the proper structural spacing, or storing fuel or other supplies... even cargo space. Though I admit, these twisted internal cavities do not look friendly for any kind of cargo we might ever carry."

"I see a lot of those bulbs," Magnus said. "I think this was a warfleet, plain and simple. No cargo ships here, at least not in this cluster of them."

"Well a lot of good it did them," Yat said. "If it was indeed that Rovan leviathan they fought, they lost rather decisively."

"Maybe," Adair said. "Or maybe the Rovan ship has repaired itself. Or maybe these ships were filled with nano-weapons that were successfully released and we're looking at a bunch of dead torpedoes."

Oh wow. If they were torpedoes… that's crazy.

"Okay, now it's just being contrary," Yat shared with Arakaki privately. Arakaki nodded. Arakaki tried to turn the last statement to her advantage.

"Excellent points," Arakaki said. "We need more information. Now we should study the Rovan ship. We can see if there's Rovans on board, check for weaknesses, learn whatever we can."

"No, no, no, we're not getting closer to that monster ship," Adair said.

"Well what do we know about it?" Arakaki demanded.

"Precious little," Magnus said. "Hiding back here in stealth mode isn't helping us scan it."

"I have an idea," Yat said. "Let's drop a few probes back here behind these hulks. Then we move away in one direction and send the probes drifting in the other. Once we've gone far enough, have the probes go active and broadcast their findings. We'll wait just long enough to receive their data, then bug out of here."

"If we get the spinner working again," Adair said.

"If?" Magnus asked.

"I think we will... I'm only trying not to set unreasonable expectations."

"Like that we might survive this?" Arakaki said.

"Exactly."

Chapter 15

Barrai sat alone on the bridge of the *Sharplight*. She sank deep into her lounge chair and watched her PV as the ship came into the Rovatick system. She watched the ship go through standard security establishment procedures. The ship spooled down its spinner and switched to sublight operation. It altered course to avoid any forces that might be trying to anticipate its position and cripple it with a strike. Then probes shot out to help the ship look for enemies.

The *Sharplight* did not appear to be in immediate danger. Barrai stayed sharp. Her training kept her alert, searching for anomalies.

Information came back from probes. The system screen displayed eight vessels near the Rovan colony planet. Six of them were already altering course to intercept the *Sharplight*.

Barrai felt a spike of adrenaline, but she handled it smoothly.

"Six contacts moving in on us," Barrai announced on the PIT channel at high priority. "I don't know how they spotted us. There may be passive sensor net in the system."

Have we found the Rovans at last? Or their enemies?

Since they were clearly spotted, Barrai launched two more probes at right angles to each other and sent off pings to get absorption patterns. If the ships were of known types, they would likely know in a few minutes.

"Get ready for a fight but veer off," Telisa said on the PIT channel.

Barrai started every ring on the ship collecting energy. She set the spinner back up a notch and brought *Sharplight* onto a new course that approximated a distant orbit around the star.

"They're maintaining an intercept course. Hostile action possible within fifteen minutes, maybe sooner."

"If they're Rovan, what's your assessment of our chances?" Telisa asked.

"Those ships are each a little larger than the ship we engaged in the binary system. That one wasn't a challenge, but with six of them, they could win. It'd be in the initial attacks, before we can knock any of them out," Barrai said.

"We should take one or two out now while we can, before that happens," Marcant urged.

Barrai waited patiently. Would Telisa give the order to attack?

No. I don't think she will.

"They don't have to be our enemies. Full retreat," Telisa ordered.

Barrai told the *Sharplight* to change course again, aiming it for the outer system. The ship did not respond as she expected. Several red warning panes flashed in her PV.

What is it? Why aren't we moving away...

"Something's wrong... we haven't changed course..."

"Figure it out fast," Telisa urged.

Barrai looked at a pane that displayed energy draw on their defensive screens. They were losing energy on the side *opposite* their enemies.

"It's a force field!" Barrai announced sharply.

"What? Out here?" Marcant asked.

"I don't know how, but it's here," she verified. "A wall that's keeping us from turning away."

Barrai suddenly realized that was exactly what had happened back at the binary system when the ship had vibrated unexpectedly. There had been a force field there, too, but much weaker. They had been fighting only one Rovan ship…

"I'm sure they're Rovan," Barrai reported.

"Blast through it! We don't want this fight," Telisa said.

Barrai told the *Sharplight* to fire through the barrier with energy weapons. The ship was fairly energy hungry, having just recently come down from the spinner's maximum capability. Barrai dropped the spinner briefly and got more rings charged.

At Barrai's command, two batteries lanced through the invisible barrier holding them in check. The *Sharplight* altered course, heading away from the star at last.

"It worked. The screen was fairly weak," she reported.

"It ought to be! There isn't a Rovan ship out here! How can they do that from so far away?"

"Maybe we should search for cloaked ships?" Marcant suggested.

Reflections from the probe pings came back. Barrai examined them in her mental battle display.

"Absorption patterns match Rovan ships," Barrai reported.

The *Sharplight* veered off course again. Barrai attempted to compensate.

"They're back at it," Barrai noted.

"Can you break through again?" Telisa asked.

"Most likely, but it may be hard to keep our rings charged if we have to keep doing this at the same time as we're defending ourselves."

"We have to bloody their noses," Marcant said.

"Break through again. Focus on disengaging," Telisa ordered.

Barrai fired on the barrier again, letting *Sharplight* slip through.

"We're through again."

Energy readings fluctuated rapidly in Barrai's PV.

Enemy fire!

The Sharplight's shields soaked a lot of energy. The ships' sensors told Barrai that despite the range, almost all of the beams coming in had struck them.

"We're being fired upon. They predicted our maneuver and used it to target their energy weapons at extreme range. Nevertheless, no damage," Barrai reported. "However, we're down even more energy."

We can win this if she wants to.

Ten seconds ticked by. Then the *Sharplight* veered yet again. Barrai felt frustration. How could they fight with the constant energy draw of breaking through the fields? And would the enemies be able to predict where the ship would be from many light seconds out by blocking them in?

"All right," Telisa said. "Turn at them. Take one of them out. Two of them if we have to."

"Aye, TM," Barrai replied.

Barrai brought the *Sharplight* up out of the system plane, then turned in at a varying angle to make the ship harder to predict at range. She chose a Rovan ship to target, the second-closest one.

The *Sharplight* cycled sixty percent of its stored energy through the weapons batteries, projecting a tight cluster of energy beams at the target ship.

A few seconds later, the light from the exploding ship reached *Sharplight*.

Barrai breathed a little easier, but when she looked at the strike analysis, she found cause for worry: the ship had *almost* survived the strike. Its shields were much stronger than any Terran vessel in that class.

"They're strong. It's a good thing we didn't try for two at once," she said.

Dozens of red dots appeared on Barrai's tactical pane in her PV.

"Missiles incoming! If you're not in a crash pod then get into one now," Barrai said.

The ship had already reserved a third of its energy rings exclusively for point defense fire and had topped them off with energy. It was all part of Barrai's battle configuration she had set up based upon her combat simulations. At this point, she had few details to worry about. The ship would enact her previously programmed decisions with superhuman timing and precision.

She leaped up from her lounge and ran to a crash tube opening on one wall of the armored bridge. She slipped in and let it close around her.

They're not firing. Which means they're holding their fire until the moment before the missiles hit our shields.

"Alpha strike is incoming. I recommend..." Barrai paused. Something was wrong. The *Sharplight*'s spinner had faltered.

"Can we disengage?" Telisa asked.

Barrai gritted her teeth. She searched through info panes related to the spinner, but no cause had been isolated.

"What? Why are we bringing down the spinner?" Telisa demanded.

"We aren't," Barrai said. "I'm searching for the malfunction."

"Pretty damn suspicious if you ask me," Marcant injected.

My thoughts exactly.

Barrai scanned the spinner system data. The system was stuck at thirty percent output, which left power for battle, but made outrunning the missiles impossible. The *Sharplight* had still not highlighted anything as the cause.

We can't run and we don't know why.

"Marcant, I need your help," Barrai said. "Can you work on the spinner problem? I need to focus on using what we've got to survive this."

That hurt.

"I'm working on it," Marcant replied rapidly.

The missiles closed steadily. They had a few minutes left. The point defense analysis pane was bright red—they did not have enough firepower to knock out all the incoming ordnance.

Barrai directed all the energy she could to the shields as the seconds ticked by. She rattled her brain for some unconventional solution.

"I'm sending four shuttles outside the ship. Maybe they can eat four missiles," Barrai said. She gave the command. The shuttles headed out for the space between *Sharplight* and its shield envelope.

That's it. That's all we have.

"Shield contact in five seconds," Barrai said.

Four... three... two...

The shields dropped completely. It was probably from enemy fire, but Barrai had no time to verify it.

All was calm.

"Nothing?" Maxsym asked.

"I—" Barrai started.

The *Sharplight* shuddered. The event was unlike any missile hit Barrai had ever experienced in simulations.

"Was that a hit? Or a near miss?" Telisa asked.

"Negative, TM," Barrai said. She started to access sensor logs of the shield breach event, but something else demanded her attention: her PV brought up new panes warning of intruders.

Many intruders.

"Intruders, lots of them," Barrai said. "Multiple hull breaches."

"They sent rovlings," Telisa concluded. "Configure internal defenses to repel them. I'll tell Magnus's robots to deploy within the ship. Everyone, prepare for personal combat."

Of course. Rovlings.

Barrai told her pod to open and leaped out.

"I don't have my OCP here," Maxsym said on the team channel.

"Marcant, get on it. Protect Maxsym until he gets his equipment."

"What? I don't have anything except a knife and my Veer suit."

"Both of you meet up and go, now," Telisa said.

Barrai had her OCP on the bridge with her. She told the ship's internal security systems to prepare for invasion with a thought. Her Veer suit was already on, so she slipped her pack on, then grabbed her cloaking sphere, breaker claw, and a PAW.

The breaker claws are usually useless against rovlings, she reminded herself.

She pulled another PAW out and slipped it over her shoulder. She looked at the small armory console before her. Forty grenades.

Should I? Hell yeah.

Barrai activated all the grenades, verified they had the team on their blacklists, gave them her rovling target sig, and told them to deploy themselves on all the approaches to the bridge. The bin came alive with spinning grenades. The orbs hopped out like a swarm of possessed billiard balls and rolled away in several directions.

Okay you creepy bastards, come on and get us then.

Barrai wanted to charge out and counterattack the invaders of her precious ship, but she sat tight and waited. The bridge provided a huge defender's advantage, with armored walls, a laser hardpoint built into the ceiling, and limited routes of access.

The Rovan ships had fallen back, as if anticipating positive results from their boarding action. Barrai split the power she had to build up the shields and take the *Sharplight* away from them.

Barrai tried to collect data about the enemy's numbers. The sensors reported twenty one hull ruptures. Some of the sites were available on video feeds, though those feeds rapidly dropped as the first rovlings emerged to attack. The inside cavities of the breacher missiles were over two meters in diameter and deep—Barrai estimated each must be eight to twelve meters deep.

That's like three hundred per tube. Over six thousand rovlings.

"I estimate enemy strength at six thousand," Barrai reported.

"How many soldier bots do we have? I know Magnus replaced our losses and then some," Telisa said.

"Three hundred."

It's not enough!

"Nine left-handed quarks! We're going to die," Marcant said.

"Do you have your OCPs yet?" Telisa demanded.

"Almost. Believe me, it's our top priority!"

"I'm headed to the nearest breach point to you two," Telisa said. "I see a group of them there. You'd better have your equipment by the time I finish that first group off."

Barrai watched Telisa in a feed from an attendant. Their leader headed into a dense group of invaders in a corridor. Her force field was on, stealth off. The rovlings opened fire immediately despite her incredible speed.

Whirr! Zing! Ping!

Telisa pressed forward.

Boom-Bang! Boom-Bang!

Telisa's shotgun launched fragmentation rounds into the midst of the vanguard, sending pieces of the rovlings flying spectacularly.

She charged the survivors, kicking them to pieces as she passed by.

Barrai was impressed at Telisa's prowess, but if the *Sharplight* had been deployed to a normal Space Force squadron, it would have a battalion of marines and assault machines aboard. Magnus's robots, while clever, lacked the raw firepower of Space Force military machines. As a result the ship was left with less internal defenses than it might have normally had.

What other weapons do I have? I can affect internal gravity, pressure, oxygen...

Barrai lifted her clenched fist and regarded it.

I'm not as fast or as strong as Telisa, but I have a force field pack and a stealth orb... and this is my ship.

Barrai hurried back to the bridge armory and grabbed two stun batons. She had seen Magnus and Telisa using them on rovlings in many simulations. She took the weapons and connected them to her Veer suit's tool clasps at her belt. She prepared the hand weapons' routines from Adair's force pack control suite. It had taken their AI a long time to figure out how to fine tune the Rovan's force field generators to allow for the use of weapons from within the protective field, but they now had the capability to use the packs with energy weapons, projectile weapons, or even the ultrasharp swords and stun batons.

"What about the spinner? What if these things are suicidal? Could they destroy the ship?" Maxsym asked on the channel.

"I doubt it, but I'll go guard the spinner," Telisa said.

"Then we'll hang out here by this armory," Maxsym said. "There's a lot of grenades and ammunition we can use."

"Good. Focus on your teamwork. Cover each other's sixes," Telisa told them.

Barrai saw that the spinner output had increased to forty percent capacity.

"We're able to disengage from the remaining Rovan ships... I think they're letting us disengage," Barrai reported.

"The Rovan ships are remotely causing the spinner problem," Marcant said. "My analysis shows that the drain is correlated with the distance between us and those Rovan ships. If we could destroy another one—"

"Keep building the distance. We have to clean house first," Telisa said.

Clean house. That's an optimistic description of our task.

Barrai checked in on the feed from one of Telisa's attendants. The PIT leader still moved through the ship incredibly fast, even with the weight of weapons and the Rovan force field generator on her back. She was almost to the main spinner assembly. She ran by a breach point in a shattered lab. A car-sized hole had been punched through the external hull of the *Sharplight*. A thick cylinder extended into the remains of the lab. Around the edges, a glistening compound had leaked through and hardened.

Our own hull repair mechanisms just sealed their cannister in place.

Telisa glanced inside. Shreds of crushed white material like packing foam littered the bottom quarter of the tube, the remains of whatever had kept the rovlings in place during transit and impact.

"They're here!" Marcant announced. Barrai saw the two scientists on the tactical, surrounded by a seething army of rovlings moving through the corridors.

Six thousand!

Barrai moved her attention away from the others' feeds as the ship's internal network warned her that a wave of rovlings had reached her outer perimeter of grenades.

Here we go.

She switched to another view and saw half a dozen rovlings darting down a corridor. The first grenade charged forward. A projectile struck it before it could close to point blank range, but it exploded anyway, focusing its concussive energy down the corridor. Before the smoke could clear, another grenade took its turn, using the smoke as cover.

Booom! Booom!

This time, the grenade made it to the feet of the lead rovlings and exploded. Barrai received its death report: five estimated kills.

Another group of rovlings pressed the bridge from a second direction. More grenades rolled out to meet them. Each grenade took out at least four rovlings, sometimes six or seven, but Barrai did not have enough.

Six thousand.

Boom! Kah-booom!

Barrai arranged the lounges for cover in the center below the laser emplacement on the ceiling. She ordered the bridge's bulkhead hatches to close.

The feed from outside her position became a chaotic view of devastation.

Booom! Booom! Ba-booom!

Her grenades rolled in time and again, wiping out rovling after rovling. Fragments of the alien machines lay in piles through the corridors. Each new blast shifted the debris around until the pieces formed rolling dunes of blackened rovling components.

Booom! Booom! Ka-thoom! Booom!

The deck shuddered. A couple of flames triggered the *Sharplight*'s fire control system, but the rovlings did not need oxygen to function. They pressed on. Soon the booms

and bangs from outside subsided to be replaced by
scraping and grinding.

Barrai how long it would take for the machines to
breach the armored doors. She told the laser emplacement
to concentrate on her flanks. The turret with the bulge
above her could spin and fire in opposite directions within
milliseconds of each other. In situations with highly
distributed targets, the turret would always spin the same
direction to minimize the need to fight the momentum of
the rotating emitter.

That left Barrai with the middle entrance facing the
bow of the ship. Behind her lay the armory and ship's best
computing cores, but they had no normal entrances. The
rovlings could likely force their way through many spaces
on the ship, but she decided to rely upon the bridge's
armor, meant to provide some protection for any Terran
officers present in battle.

Thump. Clang! Crunch!

A section of the bulkhead door to her right dented in.
Then it sundered.

Hiss! Snap!

The laser emplacement above her slagged the rovling
that tried to enter there. That did not deter the next, or the
next.

Hiss! Pop! Hisss!

Barrai took one last review of the tools at her disposal:
Veer suit, Multiple PAWs, cloaking sphere, Rovan pack,
breaker claw, two stun batons, laser pistol, four attendant
spheres, and a heavy combat knife. She also had held four
grenades in reserve.

Booom!

The central door before Barrai shattered inward. A fragment of the door almost struck her head, but it was deflected by an attendant. The orb sizzled and hurtled away, critically damaged. She was not sure if the flexible Veer helmet she had deployed would have prevented her head from being ripped off. The violence of the entrance broke her practiced calm.

That'll get the adrenaline going! Bastards!

There was no chat on the PIT channel. A quick glance to the tactical told her everyone was pressed by the invaders. Very little coordination would be possible now. Barrai raised her PAW.

Rovlings poured in. She opened fire.

Brrrrap! Brrrap! Brrrap!

The tiny rounds whizzed off and each struck one rovling in a coordinated fashion, directed by her PAW's computer. The mechanical bodies built up, then were pushed aside by a fresh wave.

Brrrrap! Brrrrap! Ching! Whirr!

The sounds of ricochets mixed in among the cacophony of combat. One rovling emerged through the fray. It had a thick armor shell. The PAW's tiny rounds, designed for ordinary rovlings, were not defeating it.

Think fast.

Barrai told her breaker claw to take it out. There was no effect. The rovling took several more steps forward.

Sonofabitch.

Brrrrap! Zing! Brrrap! Whizzzap!

She told one of her grenades to target the armored rovling. It rolled forward as Barrai tossed aside one PAW and pulled another off her back. She bent her knees, lowering her profile.

BOOOOM!

The grenade detonated just below the armored rovling, sending it flying away. Even though the majority of the grenade's force had been directed forward, there was enough backblast to shred the lounges Barrai had set up for light cover. She sent more fire into the body of rovlings headed straight in.

Brrrrap! Brrrap! Brrrap!

Suddenly the laser emplacement stopped firing. Barrai saw the error in her PV: its power ring had failed.

Something cut off its power!

Barrai had no time to contemplate the cause of its failure; now the rovlings pulled aside their fallen and massed for a new charge from all three directions.

Barrai growled like an animal. Some part of her knew it was ridiculous, but she did not have time to care. If she survived, she could joke about it later. She removed her hold on the three grenades she had left. When the charge came, the enemy would be densely packed and each could get ten kills or more.

The rovlings came for her.

Booom! Ka-Booom-Booom!

Barrai snapped on her force field and stood from her shattered cover. She let her PAW open fire furiously.

Brrraaapp!! Brrrrrappp!! Brrrrrappp!!

The weapon fired so many of its tiny rovling-killer rounds that she cleaned up the entire rovling force on her right. She swept the weapon back to the left.

Brrraaapp!! Brrrrrappp!!

The PAW ran dry. Barrai reloaded it. She heard tiny pings and saw flashes of light play across her protective field. As long as her shield held, the rovlings could not harm her.

Brrraaapp!! Brrrrrappp!! Brrrrrappp!!

Despite the devastating fire she poured out, rovlings pressed forward. Barrai could not tell the active ones from the disabled in the mess that washed across the bridge. The debris had piled up so high the doorways looked like windows.

Brrraaapp!! Brrrrrappp!!

She was out of ammunition. Barrai threw the second PAW away and pulled out her two stun batons. She told her pack to alter its force wall to place the ends of her batons outside of its protection. Rovlings charged in. Some of them were actually burrowing under their dead brethren, approaching her from under the piles.

She started swinging.

Crunch! Crackle! Whump!

At first, it felt satisfying to feel the crunch and snap of the rovlings closing on her. The alien machines shot and thrust sharp legs toward her, but they could not defeat her force field.

Soon, her arms slowed and rovlings began to surround her. She charged back toward the armory corridor to make her stand. The rovlings came at her in twos and threes through a light smoke that curtailed her vision.

Crunch! Snap! Whack!

She struggled to lift her arm and smash a rovling from the low ceiling above her in the corridor.

Should I drop these batons? I have a laser pistol. There are two more in the armory behind me...

The corridor was filled with dead rovlings. One more charged.

Whump!

She crushed it, then the baton fell from her shaking hand. A second later, her force field flickered and died.

I don't think I've even killed a thousand yet!

Barrai stood panting and fought to control her instinct to rout. Her Veer suit labored to keep her cool.

There's nowhere to run anyway, she told herself. She turned on her cloaking sphere and advanced back into the bridge. Rovlings moved by above and beside her. Her surroundings were unrecognizable in the mess and smoke. She had seen VR battles aboard Space Force ships hosting battalions that looked less shattered.

"They're thinning out," Telisa said on the team channel. "What kind of shape is the ship in? I see a lot of damage in here."

Thinning out? Is it possible?

Barrai checked her damage reports. The news was ugly: they had lost dozens of important systems nexuses. Every last laser emplacement was dead.

"Widespread damage. At least ten percent of the bastards stayed behind to destroy everything!" Barrai told them.

"Top off your ammo and charges and help me clean up the rest of them," Telisa said.

"Will do," Marcant said.

"Aye, TM," Barrai responded. If she had not been able to respond mentally over the link, she would have only emitted a dry croak.

Barrai dropped her dead Rovan pack. Losing the extra weight made her feel a little better. She staggered to one side and drew her laser pistols. The sounds of rovlings moving over the mounds of garbage surrounded her.

Barrai ran and shot like an invisible crazy person.

***

"The attack was odd," Maxsym said. He sat across from Barrai in a rovling-littered mess hall. The side of his face was bright red, having been lightly burned in an explosion.

"Odd? All of that and you come away with odd? I would have described it as deadly and scary as hell," Marcant said frantically from the next table. Barrai agreed with Marcant's sentiment, though she found him to be a bit panicky. The fight was over, but he was obviously still rattled.

Okay, maybe I'm a little rattled inside, too. But not as much as that soft hacker.

"In what way?" Telisa asked.

"Have you noticed that they don't use their greatest strength in combat? Their force fields," he answered.

"Their ships have very strong ones," Barrai said. "It took a major strike to destroy one of those ships, and it was much smaller than us."

"I mean in the intra-ship firefights. Rovlings don't use them," Maxsym said. "Even we use them. We confiscated *their* tech and adapted it for our use."

And it's a damn good thing we did, too, or the attack would have succeeded.

"Rovlings are probably too small to carry the packs," Marcant pointed out. Barrai noticed that he had a freshly repaired cut across his temple. His Veer suit's helmet lay across his shoulder; it had failed to retract properly. It was probably damaged.

"Then why didn't they make larger ones that do use them?" Maxsym said. "A sort of heavy combat rovling. After all, they have the exploding ones, and the ones with extra armor and Cthulhu knows what else."

"I don't know," Telisa said. "You have a theory, perhaps?"

"I think the force fields were made exclusively for use by the Rovans themselves," Maxsym said. "They were quite large, and the force field units we originally discovered were even heavier."

"Ah, I see. You believe the Rovans used the force fields to defend themselves against enemy rovlings," Marcant said.

Barrai nodded to herself. *Rovlings were their weapon of choice–so they had force fields to keep those things at bay.*

"There may even have been a cultural taboo against letting rovlings use them. Maybe a status thing, a kind of Rovans over rovlings mentality," Telisa said.

Well, that would put us at Rovan status. It didn't stop those damn things from trying to kill us.

"So what are we going to do about this new fleet?" Marcant asked. "It's blocked our plan."

Barrai had almost forgotten there was a plan at all. Fighting for her life and seeing the resulting destruction inside the *Sharplight* had pushed everything else out.

"The plan should change. I think there are still Rovans left alive," Barrai said. "They may have gotten a distress call from that complex."

"That's not the conclusion I would come to first," Marcant said.

"I think it's that shipyard we awakened," Telisa said. "It wants to protect the planet."

"So we're dealing with an AI, most likely," Maxsym said. "It responded to our incursion, now it's fully operational and building up the planet's defenses."

"We have to learn to talk to it. Reason with it," Telisa said. "Marcant, get on it."

Marcant smiled, but he hardly had energy to laugh.

"I mean, when you've physically recovered, of course," Telisa added.

"I've been on it for a long time now. But I'll stay on it."

"Good job getting us out of that," Telisa said to Barrai. Barrai turned to regard her commander.

"It was mostly luck. And the fact that this is a new capital ship, built with many Vovokan improvements."

"No, it was more than that. It was your abilities with *Sharplight*. If I had let you go with the others, the rest of us might not have made it."

"And now we need you to effect repairs," Maxsym said.

"All due respect TMs, we *all* need to pitch in with that, or we're not going anywhere for weeks."

Telisa nodded. "Of course, we'll all pitch in."

"Maxsym's a xenobiologist," Marcant said. "The only thing he can repair is a probabilistic quantum grid classifier."

"I'll speak for myself, thank you," Maxsym said. "But he's right."

Barrai hung her head and thought about the mountain of work before her. She was in one piece, barely, but her beloved *Sharplight* was not.

"You're a quick learner," Barrai pointed out.

Chapter 16

Yat watched the feeds of the Rovan construct as the *Iridar* crept away from the cluster of ruined ships they had examined. Their probes floated away in a rough orbit in the opposite direction.

The Rovan ship looked like a collection of four kilometer-long fuselages, oriented vertically from *Iridar*'s current vantage point. Along the central axis of the four pieces lay a thinner spine that connected them together. The spine thickened at both ends beyond the other four long components.

Yat supposed it could be a ship, but it looked like a station. Or was it simply the angle? If it was a ship that accelerated upward from his viewpoint, that would also meet Terran sensibilities of ship design. Spinner-propelled starships usually provided internal artificial acceleration parallel to the direction the spinner could pull the ship, either directly toward or away from the direction of movement.

His pane estimated the mass of the Rovan station to be 9 billion kilograms, based upon its pull on their spinner's gravity measurement systems. He shook his head.

How many things like this could be hiding out in the cold darkness between the stars across the galaxy? We only explore the systems… that was supposed to be the only place you could find anything interesting.

The probes had reached their positions for the active scan.

"Any progress with the spinner?" Arakaki said.

"No," Adair said. "I have bad news."

"The spinner is broken," Magnus guessed bravely.

"No, but it might as well be. Something external is preventing it from working. I think there's an eighty percent chance it's the gigantic ship."

"Other possibilities?" Yat asked.

"The big ship might be trapped here just like us... with some unlikely explanation I haven't seriously considered, or some radical reason I haven't even thought of."

"Back to the drawing board," Magnus said.

"I say we send the ping anyway," Arakaki said. "Those probes are distant enough now, they won't know where we are."

"But that ship will know something's going on. It will start searching," Adair said.

"Our probes could be interstellar scouts for all they know. We have to learn something," Arakaki said.

Magnus looked at Yat.

"We're stuck here. I guess the only way to get out is to learn more," Yat said.

"Here we go. Hold tight," Magnus said.

Time to poke the hive.

They waited long seconds for the energy sent from probes to reflect and come back for analysis. Finally, new data flowed into Yat's PV.

"Absorption patterns?" Arakaki asked.

"It's Rovan all right," Magnus said. "The rest of them... nothing we've seen before."

A detailed image of half the station came up in Yat's mind. He saw the intricacy of the space giant for the first time. There were sensor emplacements, hatches, and cone-shaped stations scattered across its surface.

Probably hull breach repair modules? Force field projectors?

160

Yat found the weapons. There were hundreds of energy projectors. The surface also held dozens of large bay doors.

That thing could have a hundred other ships inside of it. And a million rovlings. More.

"That thing is made for war," Magnus stated.

Yat looked at the leviathan in his PV and had to agree.

***

On the next shift, Yat sat close to Arakaki in a small mess on the Vovokan *Iridar*. Magnus sat across from them and Adair stood in the entranceway.

"That's it then," Arakaki said. "We learn about this race we think are the enemies of the Rovans. If they were strong enough to break the Rovans, they're a danger to Terrans, too."

"Sounds like a good use of our time," Magnus said, though his voice lacked conviction.

"We have nothing to lose," Arakaki said.

"We could wait for the *Sharplight* to show up," Magnus said.

"I think it would take more than that. Like a combined Terran-Celaran task force, or a couple of Vovokan battleships," Adair said. "Worse, if *Sharplight* shows up, it probably won't be able to hide like this Vovokan ship. It might get carved into pieces like all these other ships."

Magnus sat across from them, eating chunks of some synthetic fruit.

"We don't know which side caused the war," he pointed out.

Arakaki shrugged. "We need to know more about *any* potential enemy."

Yat nodded. "I'm in. If we have to wait here for help anyway, we need to find what we can before *Sharplight* shows up. Maybe we could learn something that would keep them alive."

"Okay. We'll head for the nearest cluster of dead ships," Magnus said. "We'll make it a point to note any weaknesses in either race we can find. It would be interesting to know how they fought each other. That might help us if we have to face either or both as enemies."

Both! Now that would be bad.

Yat looked at Magnus's planned course in his PV. The ship eased toward a group of fifty chunks of debris that might have been a squadron of thirty alien ships hundreds or thousands of years ago. The slow-moving *Iridar* would arrive within range of an expedition in an hour.

"Gear up," Magnus said. "We'll use real space suits and our OCPs."

Yat knew that their Veer suits, while equipped with extendable helmets and a modest oxygen supply, were not designed for extended use in space. Momma Veer had merely provided for temporary protection in case of depressurization of a starship.

"Our Rovan force field packs have only been configured for use with Veer suits," Arakaki pointed out. "Aren't the space suits considerably bulkier?"

"I'll handle that part," Adair said. It was Adair who had figured out how to shape the force fields for their use in the first place.

Yat could not help but feel a spike of anxiety as he thought about Adair preparing a new configuration. He could not shake the memory of what had happened to Oliver. Nevertheless, he followed Arakaki to a set of lockers where they had stowed their gear upon arriving at the new ship. The *Iridar* told Yat that the Terran space suits were available at either of two airlock prep rooms. He grabbed his gear and a PAW from the locker.

"I know what you're thinking," Arakaki told him. "Don't worry. If the force field crushes you, I'll shoot Adair for you."

Yat smiled bravely, though her comment hit a nerve. Oliver had been his friend and had died right next to him.

She's seen more death than you have. She became callous to it.

"How are we going to wear these packs with the space suits? They're supposed to go on the outside of our Veer suits," Yat asked.

Yat had used space suits in VR training, but he had never done one with a combination of the Rovan field packs and a space suit in tandem.

"Keep it on the outside," Arakaki told him. "The space suits have room for packs, too. The suit designers knew that there were many different missions to be performed in space, so they have back mounts for all kinds of equipment."

"Okay, but the pack will be ten centimeters farther out on your back," Yat said. "It may make it awkward to maneuver."

"Yeah, but it's zero-g anyway, so your attendants will realign you if necessary."

Magnus, Arakaki and Yat walked to the starboard lock. He saw from the navigation map that they were almost upon the reef of dead ships.

"Let's try that one. It looks intact. Most of these others are in pieces," Arakaki said. Yat checked her pointer on the tactical and found the ship she indicated.

"It's warm," Yat pointed out. "I mean, the outside is barely radiating low frequency radiation, but that ship isn't as cold as the others."

"Why do you suppose the Rovans didn't notice that and finish them off?" Arakaki asked.

"We don't know for sure that Rovan ship did all this," Magnus said.

"Awww, c'mon. It did," Yat said.

Magnus nodded. "I agree it feels likely. But if Telisa were here, you know she'd be warning us against building on a mountain of assumptions."

"Okay, the working theory is that they fought the Rovan battleship and these are the losers. That theory would mean the Rovans want all these ships destroyed. Why not break this one in half like the others? It's still warm, they didn't kill it utterly. That weakens our theory."

"Maybe this one is only playing dead," Yat said excitedly.

"Given that thought, you still want to check it out?" Magnus asked.

"Yes!" Arakaki answered for Yat.

Magnus mulled it over for a second.

"Okay. Everyone have lots of weapons?"

***

164

Yat, Arakaki, and Magnus exited a lock of the *Iridar* into the cold of space. The distances were even greater than usual: they were now in the void between stars. The thought made him nervous.

What difference does it make? he told himself. *A light second or a light year from safety, either way, without a ship you're dead.*

Yat's attendants nudged him toward the alien ship. His space suit had maneuvering capability, but the team had decided to conserve their reactant. The silence of the void might have been creepy if Yat was not already used to it from their constant VR training sessions.

They alighted on the dead alien shape. The surface had been decorated with long spiral lines that looked like the curving trajectories of subatomic particles after a collision.

Is that art? Functional? Identification?

Magnus led them twenty meters along the surface and halted. He pointed at an apparent hatch or panel in the surface of the alien hull.

"Here we are again. The eternal problem. How to open an alien door," Magnus said.

"You have me on the team now," Yat said confidently. "I'll get it open."

Yat had brought his full incursion pack. These were not Rovan ships, so he would be starting from scratch. The idea excited him. This was his specialty: cracking safes and security hardpoints. Though his skills had, until recently, only involved Terran obstacles, he had often had to apply out-of-the-box thinking to defeat many security systems. He credited that mode of thinking for his success with Rovan doors, though he had since then learned that the Rovans were remarkably naive at security.

Yat's attendants scanned the hairline crack in the hull. Their information formed up in his PV. The hull was less dense along the crack, implying that there might be some open space behind the edges. There were no signs of hinges or any denser connections to the surrounding hull. The door itself, however, had complex components at its center, implying some kind of electronic system.

Okay, so it has a brain. Why no hinges? There's no lower density area indicating a pocket for it to slide out of the way...

"This will take time," Yat said. "I'm not embarrassed to say, it would help if Adair could assist me. It might be able to make sense of these scans, help me guess which of these structures are related to the door, and how to activate them."

"No rush. We don't have any plans for lunch," Arakaki said.

"Lay it on me," Adair said. Yat sent a pointer to the information.

Yat resumed puzzling through what he saw.

No hinges. No slider spaces. So, it's held in place what, magnetically? Or is this not a door at all? Could it be an artifact of the building process, just a panel in the hull?

Yat checked the magnetic fields. They were all very small and weak, mostly around the area of the suspected brain of the door. He had no idea how to manipulate the brain. Yat typically opened things not by hacking the brain, but by fooling the simpler components that the brain commanded. It was easier to convince the dumb parts that the brain had told them to do something.

Yat got a small rod out of his pack. It was a tool he had used many times before on Terran portals. One end of the rod had a flat disk, which he placed against the hull.

"Uhm, are you getting ready to… what is that thing?" Magnus asked nervously.

"This is an electrochemical adherer. This disk surface changes to mimic a type of glue appropriate to match the molecules it's placed against. Then I put stress on the rod, and watch how the surface underneath reacts at a microscopic level. It tells me how stiff the material is, and if it flexes even just a little bit, the flex pattern across the entire surface can give clues about the anchor points that are behind it."

"I love it when you talk dirty," Arakaki said.

Yat let his adherer match up, then he hit the rod a few times on its side. Another window came up in his PV. The flex pattern was uniform based upon distance from an outside edge. He tried the adherer on two more spots and got the same result.

"It's affixed all along the edge equally," he said. "Either that, or the door is so well made that its stresses are perfectly distributed along its entire surface."

"I think it's sealed all along the edge," Adair said.

"That's bad news," Arakaki said. "It sounds to me like this is a section of the hull they sealed up last when they were done making the ship."

"Maybe," Adair said. "If it is a door, it probably either goes straight in or straight out. Most likely the latter."

"I agree," Yat said. "But we can't reset it or somehow shock the system into opening because as an external hull hatch, it will default to staying in place in any unusual circumstance."

"I need to try and cut in to learn more about what it's like on the border," Yat said.

Magnus nodded.

Yat took out a powerful laser scalpel and a micropick. He floated over to the hairline crack and started cutting. It took him fifteen minutes to get through the durable compounds of the alien hull. Once he had a hole burned through the outer surface, he slid the micropick through the tiny hole and took a sample. Then he retrieved the pick and put the sample into another machine.

Yat examined the substance he had pulled out at a microscopic level. He saw long, contractile fibers and a series of very thin conductors that branched out into it. He asked for a conductivity analysis.

"This substance acts as a memory muscle," he announced. "At 'rest' it expands, but when these artificial nervous pathways are activated, it contracts."

"Allowing the door to open," Adair concluded.

"You have it figured out?" Arakaki asked.

"I think so. The outside of the door has a slot all the way around. This substance is wedged into it, keeping the door in place. We can induce currents inside the border of the door and get it to contract. The trick will be figuring out what kind of currents."

Yat took out a thick loop of flat material and attached it to the hull around the edges of the door. Once it was in place, he generated a changing magnetic field. At first, he tried to induce very small currents. Nothing happened.

"Adair, can you suggest some waveforms to try?"

"Sure."

Yat looked up at Magnus and Arakaki.

"Give us some more time. We just have to get it right…"

The door moved outward. Yat pushed himself off the hull hurriedly. He told his attendants to help pull him back.

The door came a few centimeters out of the hull, then moved sideways along the outside surface.

"Weird. The door detached completely and floated along the hull to there!" Arakaki said.

An attendant took a peek at the door. It was in contact with the hull, but there were no runners or slots. As far as they could tell, the door had just floated up and out of the way.

Magnus shined his weapon's light into the opening.

"There's no lock," he observed. "It goes straight in there."

"No pressure inside. That means, no crew, right?" Arakaki guessed.

"Maybe they didn't need atmosphere, but yeah, more evidence that it's robotic," Magnus said.

"There may be battle damage we haven't noted that emptied the ship," Adair pointed out.

"Be careful. If it has defenses, we'll be likely targets," Arakaki said.

"We look nothing like rovlings, at least," Yat pointed out.

"Yes, but a robotic ship would be more likely to assume we're enemies, given the locale and circumstances," Magnus said.

Magnus activated his force pack and floated into the opening.

Arakaki did not follow him.

"It might close on us," she said.

Michael McCloskey

"I'll have a soldier stand there," Magnus said from within. One of his robots crept along the ornate hull and stopped in the doorway.

Arakaki activated her protective field and slipped by into the alien ship. Yat grabbed his gear and did the same.

Yat kept his attention forward. As Magnus had said, there was no second hatch in sight. He paused to examine the interior while keeping some attention on Magnus's video feed from the front. Both spots were similar: the interior was a fragmented collection of jagged surfaces, each one covered with sharp ridges of material that ran like inscribed mazes everywhere he could see. Deep, narrow gaps broke the walls every few meters. The gaps absorbed his light, making it hard to resolve anything within.

"I can't tell what is wall and what might be... equipment or tools or anything," Arakaki said.

"I think it's just another indication this ship had no crew," Yat said.

The team navigated to a new section of the ship, propelled by their attendants. The passageway they had taken was, in turn, a gap in the jagged wall of a larger space.

"This ship is crazy," Yat whispered.

The corridor before them looked like a work of fractal art. The ceiling was the simplest: a flat plane supported by seven wandering beams. The supports were spaced wide starting on the left as they faced starboard, but the spaces between beams shrank steadily as they were placed until the rightmost beams were close together. The beams and the ceiling all looked to be one piece of seamless material.

The walls had a repeating series of gaps like the one they had emerged from that grew slowly narrower as the corridor proceeded forward. The floor held three-meter-long grooves placed seemingly at random. The space shrank and curved off toward their right, what Yat had thought of as the aft of the vessel.

"It's like being inside a nautilus shell, except... with lots of armholes in its shell," Arakaki said.

Yat had a horrible thought.

"What if the Rovan ship has some weapon that… *melted* the insides of these ships? Maybe what we're looking at is a slagged interior."

"Like we're standing where a bubble of hot gases or plasma erupted inside a shell of molten metal?" asked Arakaki.

"I doubt it," Adair said. "The interiors are too uniformly formed, and we see signs of more conventional battle damage on the other wrecks. Though I admit I'm not sure. I suppose it's possible some unknown attack form could have done this."

They floated forward. Yat let his attendants carry him gently along. The curve of the open space straightened and opened. The slots on the walls halted to be replaced by grooves like the floor had; the walls leaned inward above their heads until they joined in a peak, ending the flat part of the ceiling.

Still no furniture, controls, or equipment… that I can identify or understand.

"Now less like a nautilus now and more like a... okay is this art or a functional design?" Arakaki demanded, giving up on finding a new comparison.

"Soooo weird. That twisty part behind us was probably the aft," Magnus said, focusing at the tactical. "Then it leads here and has three main sections."

"Okay, well, where's the heat coming from?" Arakaki asked.

"Everyone, send an attendant to find it," Magnus ordered. They each sent one of their three attendants out to scout the bizarre corridors.

The tactical map grew. The inside of the ship looked like a map of a narrow reservoir with several rivers feeding it and hundreds of intricate coves littered along its edge. Yat did not see any signs of danger on the map or in the video feeds.

"Found it," Magnus said, though Yat had already noticed it on the tactical.

"Stay alert," Arakaki warned. "The heat could be from an alien. It or the ship defenses might lash out when we approach."

They marched to the spot in single file. Yat kept his head on a pivot, but the environment was so alien he did not know if he would recognize danger before it was too late.

When they arrived, an attendant circled the a three-meter tall cylinder in a gentle descending spiral, taking readings. The cylinder was covered in thick ridges and spikes. Rather than rising straight upward, it leaned about fifteen degrees to one side, but its solid anchoring to floor and wall showed that it had been constructed that way.

"It's a tank of liquid," Arakaki announced, reviewing the attendant's findings. "Something has kept it warm."

"I wonder what it is," Magnus said. "No high frequency radiation is escaping. Just the infrared. Only weak magnetic fields..."

"Well, how can we find out? There's no way we're prying this thing out of here and taking it back with us," Arakaki said.

"My medikit has a field analyzer," Yat said. "If we can get in there, maybe we can figure out what it is."

Arakaki shrugged. "Sure, give it a try."

Magnus and Yat approached the structure. Yat found a footing in one of the nearby gaps and scooted himself halfway up the alien device.

"Here," Magnus said, pointing at a depression near the top. Yat found a similar depression on his side, along a barely discernible line. Each was a slot inset into the surface, less than a centimeter wide.

"It's a lid. These might be... for some tool to grab and lift it? Or to release it."

Yat fumbled with the lid with his force pack on. His fingers could not grasp the lid unless he turned it off.

"I'm deactivating my pack," he announced.

Arakaki looked at him sharply, but she said nothing. *She knows we have to take risks. At least she looks concerned.*

Yat's force field came down. His hands grasped the top of the device, which was twice as thick as his torso. There were three of the slots. Each of his hands got a finger into the slot and tried to lift. Nothing happened.

"I'll get this side," Magnus offered.

Suddenly the top of the device popped up. Yat almost lost his balance. He dropped the lid from his left hand and grabbed the edge of the opening. The lid flopped, held only in his right hand and struck the edge of the device. He could feel the clang through his suit but no sound came since the ship had no air.

He leaned forward and peeked into the opening. It was a hollow tank below, three-quarters filled with greenish liquid.

"What you got there? Alien brain in a jar?" asked Arakaki.

"It looks like green slime. Hold the lid, please," Yat said. Magnus stabilized the lid from his side.

"Green slime," Arakaki echoed. "We're trapped in a bad VR."

Yat took out his analyzer and waved it over the liquid. He accessed the device through his link. Panes opened in his PV as the machine ran its tests. One pane came to the fore in his mind. A microscopic ovoid trailing cilia came into view.

"Yapzers."

"What is it?" Magnus asked.

"There are… I'm going to call them cells," Yat said.

"Maxsym can figure it out. Just make sure we keep it isolated until we can figure out if it's dangerous," Magnus said.

Yat nodded. He quickly sealed the container. He felt a rush. They worked to get the lid back on the tank.

Is this what it's like to discover a new form of alien life?

Yat decided he could get used to being a PIT team member.

Chapter 17

Telisa paced about on the battle-scarred deck of the *Sharplight.*

This has to be the result of our meddling at the Rovan complex. For a thousand years these places lay dormant… now, they've come back to life?

She took another walk around the perimeter of the briefing hall. Three rows of empty seats faced her. A long, blank wall stretched behind her. A row of smashed refreshment servers littered another.

Could the Rovans have some kind of natural hibernation cycle? Maybe their home planet had a highly elliptic orbit...

Marcant and Maxsym showed up together. They sat down in a couple of seats. Within another minute, Barrai walked in. She looked grim. Telisa did not know if it was because of her assignment to the ship with those who had disagreed with her, or the magnitude of the repairs they undertook. Despite Barrai's countenance, Telisa knew she could trust Barrai to act professionally.

"How are repairs going?" Telisa asked. She had helped to repair a few minor systems herself, but most of the *Sharplight* was beyond her expertise.

"Fair," Barrai said. "Mostly thanks to automated repair processes, we're at eighty percent battle efficiency, but don't let that fool you. That metric is a measure of our effectiveness in the middle of a war. The *Sharplight* 'fixes' many of its systems automatically, but they're meant to be repairs to get the ship ready to return to battle. They're a far cry from meaning that everything's back to the way it was before. The ship's skeleton is good, the energy system lines are back in place, but we're missing whole rooms. In a few places there's no deck to walk on. A lot of our convenient link services are gone."

"We'll live with it and keep at it," Telisa said.

"For the record, Maxsym's not half bad at fixing things," Barrai added.

Telisa smiled. Then she returned to the new agenda she had in mind for the meeting.

"How much you want to bet our Vovokan shuttles are stealthy enough to get through that blockade?" Telisa asked her team.

"Not our lives," Barrai said.

"I can fly a shuttle out. We'll be able to tell if they know I'm there," Telisa maintained. "I'll have time to bug out if they detect me."

"Do those biosupply modules even fit on a shuttle?" Marcant asked.

"Possibly," Maxsym said. "But we pulled over fifty empty ones from S3. It'll take many to resupply even one station."

"Well, the Rovans had to be shipping those things out, right? Maybe the colony still has—"

"We didn't find any spaceships until one came out of that base!" Marcant objected.

"Well, they have spaceships now, don't they?"

"I'm coming with you," Marcant said.

Telisa did a double take.

Did he just say—

"What?" demanded Telisa.

"Are you serious?" Maxsym asked. "Barrai, talk some sense into them please."

"Keep your eyes peeled for any evidence of living Rovans," Barrai urged Marcant. "Find out if that base is producing these ships!"

Maxsym sighed.

"I'm surprised you're signing up for this," Telisa said to Marcant.

"You'll need me to get in there and stay hidden. Your physical prowess will only get you so far," he said.

Hidden agenda? Or has Marcant become valiant?

Telisa supposed it might not be so valiant coming from a simulationist.

Could it even be he wants to be alone with me while Magnus is gone?

Telisa gave it a second's thought.

Nah.

"Actually this body has a sharpened mind, too," Telisa said, though she knew Marcant's help would be valuable. Hacking alien systems a specialty of his.

Marcant held up his hands.

"*Please* let me help. I want to get what we need to revive the Rovans! Imagine what we'll learn," he said passionately.

"Oh, I've imagined it, alright. I'm as eager as you two," Telisa said. She turned to Marcant. "Gear up."

***

Telisa and Marcant settled into the shuttle.

"You pack lighter than Maxsym," she said.

"I've got what I need."

"This is going to be a long journey under full stealth restrictions," Telisa said. "Days."

"It'll be worth it," Marcant maintained, still completely self-assured.

Telisa nodded. She told the shuttle to exit the *Sharplight* and hide itself.

"Well, we have plenty of time to hone the plan," she said.

"What plan?"

"Exactly."

Marcant drew a deep breath and leaned back in his seat.

"So, to sum it up, we need to first, locate a biosupply module, two, get it out of whatever complex it's in, three, load it into this shuttle, and four, fly back to the *Sharplight*. All undetected," Marcant said.

"Your thinking is too rigid," Telisa criticized.

"What? I was just getting started."

"Too many initial assumptions in your outline. You're thinking too small."

"Oh? Show me an example of big, flexible thinking," Marcant said.

"We sneak in there, find *all* the modules we need, load them up onto a *Rovan* ship and take off with them," Telisa said.

"Perspicacious," Marcant said. "Except that the planet is largely devoid of spacecraft, remember?"

"Then we should probably penetrate the complex that's making the ships like I suggested in the first place," Telisa said.

"You do know that my skills with Rovan stuff is at the open-a-door level, right?"

"You're going to learn more on this trip."

"It stands to reason that the complex we kicked will be heavily watched and guarded."

"It's the only shipyard we know of on the planet," Telisa said. "In fact, I feel pretty sure it's the only one there. Most of the complexes were simple storage sites for colony supplies. So your first order of business is to go through all of our data collected from the Rovatick system. We need to check and see if any of the things we investigated matched these empty biosupply modules we transported out of S3."

"Ah. Good idea. We might have already seen some!"

"It'll be a little harder than just looking for a target signature of the opened ones we have. We saw a lot of crates and containers in a lot of places. We'll need to match containers of those dimensions as well."

"Including multiples of that size, in all dimensions," Marcant pointed out.

"Right. Good to see you already attacking the problem," she said.

***

The stealthed shuttle flew low over the field of green streamers. They came over a rocky rise and saw the military complex the team had narrowly escaped from.

"Is this even the same place?" Marcant asked, aghast.

A kilometer-wide field had been cleared around the entrance to the underground complex. Dozens of the huge Rovan land vehicles were parked in rows to one side. On the other side, palettes of supplies were stacked ten meters high. Rovlings transported materials into the complex. The wounds in the landscape caused by *Sharplight's* attack had been filled in with low towers of dark ceramic. Telisa spotted several upward-facing hangar doors that could only exist to allow small spacecraft in and out of the complex.

"Any Rovans?" Telisa demanded.

Marcant returned to his study of the shuttle's sensor data.

"No..." he eventually answered, though he was clearly still looking.

Telisa saw something else of interest.

"There's the shipyard's original exit point," Telisa said, pointing out a huge set of complex carbon doors set into a massive hexagonal frame of heavy ceramics.

"Even if they've been making ships nonstop, I doubt you're going to find a transport ship just sitting around," Marcant said.

"We'll see. First, we verify the suspected bio modules stashed in that bay."

"Okay. I'll take us down a half klick past the new perimeter."

Telisa steeled her mind for her return to the shipyard complex. She felt the shuttle stir under her as Marcant told it to land.

"You know, we could learn a lot about the Rovans by studying their AI here," Marcant mused. "Think about it. Everything on this planet was all wrapped up and waiting for Rovan colonists. This complex was its sole shipyard and, apparently, military presence. Then we went in there and stirred it all up. Now it's mobilized and producing a fleet. I also saw new constructs on the ground. Defenses, I bet."

"There might be a real Rovan down there somewhere, but I tend to agree it's probably an AI. So what does this teach us? The Rovans are efficient? They don't waste resources on defense until it becomes necessary?"

"At the very least I think it points to them not being inherently warlike," Marcant said. "Also, it might mean that they've encountered hostiles before. Either other Rovan factions, or aliens. This is a big response. I feel like all this had been prepared for, but not implemented until it became necessary."

Telisa frowned. Marcant had reminded her that he was probably the reason the entire thing had gone south. He caught her gaze.

"I'm sorry I caused the alarm. I was intensely curious. Look, I'm down here risking my white buttocks with you now—"

"We all make mistakes," Telisa said. "Yours have been very visible ones, very impactful, but that's because your role is so critical to us. You have your hands into more things that most of us, so your mistakes come up more often."

Marcant nodded gratefully.

"Now, let's quit yapping and get out there. You have your full OCP?"

"Cloaking orb, breaker claw, force field pack, yep. All charged."

"Okay. Minimum communication. I know the Celarans have set up our cloaking systems very well, but we know the Rovans have strong detection capabilities if we give them reason to become suspicious."

Which we are about to do by moving supplies and stealing a ship.

The shuttle door opened. Telisa found the light of the star familiar.

"On me," she said. She activated her Celaran orb and strode out. One glance behind revealed Marcant had done the same. Their orbs coordinated, allowing her PV to paint him as a faint green outline in her vision. The shuttle looked like a clump of streamer-plants in her normal vision, but her PV overlayed a green glow in the true shape of the shuttle.

Telisa cut her way through the streamers near their landing site and found a rocky patch leading toward the Rovan facility. The two PIT members continued on into the developed area among the Rovan vehicles that looked vaguely like yachts on wheels.

A few rovlings scuttled along purposefully through the area. Telisa avoided them as best she could while keeping their heading for the original ground gate into the complex. The sound of their passing was dampened by the Celaran cloaking technology, though they left some light footprints behind.

Of course a cloaking orb designed for a flying creature wouldn't clean up footprints. I need to ask our team on Blackhab to make a Terran version that can do that.

When they arrived at the gate, she found that it looked much the same as before. She warily noted a sensor cluster above the entrance. Marcant moved around her in total silence. She kept her eyes on the rovlings she saw as he started to work. So far, it did not appear that any alarms had been tripped.

Telisa waited patiently. She wanted a report, but reduced communications would help to ensure their safety. She watched the surface for several minutes.

Finally the hatch opened. Telisa strode through as a series of rovlings marched out, pulling long wheeled platforms. She wondered if Marcant had gotten them in at all, but it did not matter. They were in.

The corridor beyond was white and clean, lit from above by a gentle glow. Telisa took the lead again. They retraced their path from last time they had been in the complex, but soon came to a new area. The white corridor expanded into a new room filled with stacks of containers. Rovlings worked to move the cargo out through a dozen tubes.

This facility needed to increase its ability to take raw materials shipments to keep up with the production of ships, Telisa decided.

She oriented herself on the tactical, which showed the old complex map and their current location.

The old warehouse with the ceiling doors had been far to her left. Telisa moved in that direction, looking for a way to get back on track. She found a Rovan-sized corridor that went the correct direction and took it.

They came to the wide intersection with interlocking geometric shapes on the floor. The center statue was exactly as she recalled it, a spiral column of ten-sided shapes rising from the floor to a low ceiling. She wondered again what it meant to a Rovan.

Ah, back on familiar territory.

She selected the passage that Yat and Oliver had taken up to the bay-warehouse. There, the attendants had recorded hundreds of containers, some of which matched a multiple of the size of the bio supply modules they sought.

A column of rovlings met them in the corridor, moving in the opposite direction. Telisa quickly stepped aside and crouched in the triangular side-section of the corridor where the rovling tubes often joined main passageways. The rovlings scuttled on past her.

She looked over at Marcant's sensor ghost as the alien machines receded. He had copied her motion, though he sat between two open rovling tubes.

Cutting it close.

She resumed her course up to the bay. They arrived within another minute of hurried sneaking.

The ceiling doors were open. Light shone down onto two alien transports and hundreds of cargo containers. As at the other room, rovlings carried supplies into the complex.

Uh oh. They may have cleared out the bio supply modules. What need would they have for those to make their defense squadron?

Telisa walked toward the edge of the bay where the suspected modules had been placed. She saw row after row of larger containers. Some dust blew across the floor, not too surprising given the wide-open doors above. The containers looked new.

She came to the next-to-last row by the far side of the bay and turned into the stacks. One… two… three stacks in.

There!

The same container that Yat and Oliver had scanned was still in its place.

The box matched the depth and height of a biosupply module, with double the width. Telisa stopped and prepared to break into it. Marcant's ghost walked over and knelt beside it. Telisa checked herself; she supposed he would convince the container to open quietly. It took the simulationist about thirty seconds to open it.

Within, Telisa saw exactly what she had hoped: two biosupply modules, side by side. The gray containers had a series of about a dozen circular caps scattered across the top where the contents could be filled or drained. She moved close to Marcant's ghost so that her directional transmissions would be weak, low-frequency whispers in the electromagnetic spectrum.

"Our first objective is complete. Now we need to find an appropriate ship, or we're going to have to pull this off a dozen times," Telisa said.

"I appreciate optimism, but I think your Trilisk-designed brain is running over with it. I feel like if we make a single mistake in here, we'll be ripped to pieces."

Telisa shrugged, then realized her gesture might be lost with her stealth on. They moved out silently to look for transport.

Telisa thought of the huge rotating door they had traveled through before. It seemed likely that any starships within the complex would be beyond one of those portals. That meant a high chance of being discovered, and once beyond such a hardpoint, if they were detected, it would likely block their exit route.

Telisa had had time to contemplate that problem. She had come up with two possible solutions: one, perhaps they could drop into the complex at the top of the shaft where the completed vessels emerged; that still left a problem of getting the biomodules loaded up.

Her second idea, inspired by the fleet build up, was that they could follow the flow of raw materials into the complex to the ships being built. Surely the raw materials flowing into the station could not all fit through the narrow rovling tubes? And moving those supplies through the rotating security doors would be too slow.

They walked the perimeter of the bay. In the rear of the warehouse, three large sets of metal doors had been set into the ceramic wall. Telisa saw something new on the floor in front of each portal: metal rails built into the floor.

Okay, there it is. The materials that come in by air are moved down into the shipyard. We should be able to follow them in. Or, worst case scenario, climb into a container and get a ride.

Telisa stood by the nearest of the doors and waited. Marcant understood the objective and worked on the door. Soon it opened. Telisa peered beyond.

The rail led down in the center of a wide corridor. To either side, a narrow raised walkway provided room for rovlings. The walkways were sloped but had pronounced ridges every half meter or so. Telisa supposed the rovlings might provide the motive force for the rail cars or platforms that moved up and down the rails. The ridges could provide plenty of traction for the rovlings working the cars.

She entered the cargo tunnel. The slope was gentle, perhaps ten degrees. The tunnel darkened as they descended in silence. It continued for over a hundred meters before Telisa saw a new feature ahead.

A small station had been built on the left side of the rails. The rails split left in two spots, allowing cargo on the way down to be diverted to the station.

Telisa decided to investigate, even though her link told her that the shipyard was still far ahead and below their current position. She hopped off the narrow walkway and sized up the station. She saw a raised platform to her right and a wide doorway on her left. Bright bars of light shone from above.

She took a step toward the raised platform. Its side had a series of seams. Suddenly she realized it was a stack of flat sleds. She decided the sleds probably slid or floated up and took cargo down the corridor... to where?

Marcant had been working on the door. When it opened, Telisa started down the corridor. The passageway had the now-familiar design of a clear, white main run with angled alcoves to either side that made the floor twice as wide as the ceiling. Rovling pipes joined the corridor at random every five or ten meters, emptying into the alcove area.

Marcant followed silently. The corridor split at a four-way intersection after twenty meters, then split again after another twenty. Each time she strode straight ahead. She passed several smaller narrow doors until the corridor branch she had taken ended in a large square portal.

This looks important.

Marcant opened the door. A large, brightly-lit bay lay beyond. They sneaked inside.

Nestled within, a Rovan ship floated over a meter above the ground. It was at least ten times larger than their shuttle. The vessel looked brand new. Telisa could not see any kind of loading ramp or walkways into the ship. She supposed being Rovan, it could probably use force fields to give access to any part of the vessel from below.

She peered upward, looking for the exit path. The bay rose over a hundred meters. A white ceiling capped the top. It was hard to tell the exact distance to the top, even with her superb vision. Was that distant ceiling part of a doorway, or did the bay join a horizontal tunnel far above? The ship had to emerge from the complex somehow.

Once again, she stepped close to Marcant's green ghost.

"That was easy! It's big enough to hold our modules," Telisa transmitted.

"Easy to *find*. We haven't seized it. Why isn't it being used to bring in materials too?" Marcant asked.

"Not sure. Maybe this planet has plenty of natural resources. They don't need to ship much in from other planets," Telisa said. "I need control of that ship."

"There's a chance that the ship will notice me. Then we can assume the AI will know we're here…"

And this time, the Sharplight is too far away to help us.

"Leave me your hacking suite and get back to the shuttle. I'll take it from here," she said.

"No! That's not what I meant. I'm just trying to set expectations here. This is a *starship*. Rovan or not, I would probably need time and isolation from negative consequences to figure it out."

"Isolation from negative consequences? Not going to happen," she said. "Do your best. Take your time if you have to. It'll be a while before we can get all those biomodules loaded up."

Marcant did not reply. Telisa understood exactly what he was saying, but she also knew Marcant was a genius. Properly motivated, he might surprise himself.

It's not like I'm asking him to hack a Vovokan ship.

"Let's set up an abort ping that's unlikely to be picked up," Telisa said. She synced their cloaking spheres so they could exchange a low frequency signal in case of trouble. The signal looked like noise; it served only as a flag that they needed to bail on the operation.

Marcant's digital silhouette stirred.

"This is almost impossible," Marcant said. "First we have to hack this ship, then two sets of bay doors to let the ship out, then we have to open the cargo area doors to let us back in, load the modules up, open the cargo area doors yet again and fly away. I've spent months on projects simpler than this, and that was working against Terran systems, not alien ones."

"I agree, that's too complex. I'll load the ship where it is. Then, you open this bay's doors just one time and we're out of here. We'll leave our shuttle behind."

"Okay. How do we move all those crates? Oh, I forgot. You're stronger than six of me."

"Actually, I was thinking we would have a robot do it."

"Maybe," Marcant said. "The doors are kind of black magic. We have effective methods, but we don't know that much about what we're working with. Yet."

"Okay, focus on the ship. I'll use one of the sleds. Maybe."

A hatch opened in the ship hovering over them.

"Not sure how I'm going to get up there," Marcant said.

189

"You'll figure it out. Know your escape route just in case."

Telisa turned back the way they had come. She considered running and rejected the idea. Marcant would need time to work. Even if she had to bring the biomodules down one at a time, she would still likely end up waiting on him.

She eyed a door as she walked by.

Should I poke around? No. We have an important mission.

Telisa returned to the railside loading dock and strode back up on the walkway. A rumbling noise came to her sharp ears. Something was coming. Likely, a load of cargo.

A flat cargo car as wide as the tunnel between the walkways came into sight above. It was loaded with cargo containers. Three rovlings braked the cargo car on either side from the walkway.

Telisa remained fully cloaked, but the procession still presented a problem. There would be no room on her walkway, or the one on the other side. She glanced at the angled ceiling. It offered no purchase.

Telisa relaxed her muscles and waited. As the rovlings and the cargo palette bore down on her, she bent her legs and prepared to spring. The cargo car rumbled closer. As it approached within five meters, Telisa leaped.

Time slowed as she hurtled through the air. Her arms reached forward and met the front of a container. Her hands wrapped the edge, thumbs down the front and fingers over the top, as if she intended to do diamond pushups against the edge. Her body slid forward in the air and the cart continued below, combining their velocity.

She allowed her arms to bend and tucked her head slightly to the right. As she flew over the cargo, she rolled her right shoulder across the top. Her legs came over, her feet planted, then she pushed off.

Telisa flew off the top of the cargo on the other side and landed on all fours onto the walkway beyond the cargo cart and its rovlings.

The entire thing had only taken a second. It would have occurred in the flash of an eye for any normal Terran. Telisa straightened back up and inhaled.

That felt good.

Telisa hurried up the tunnel. Though she had decided Marcant needed time, she did not want to risk having to pass another cargo car. She emerged from the door at the top.

Another railcar waited near one of the other doors. She was not sure how to direct it over to her door.

Hrm. If I just pull the container down the rails… what will happen if another car is coming up?

Telisa decided to cross that bridge later. She stalked down the stacks back to the biosupply modules. When she found the modules, she looked around for rovlings or any obvious sensor emplacements nearby. Seeing none, she picked up the module. It was ungainly, and heavy, but her host body managed it. She put it in the aisle and slid it toward the doors.

Telisa moved slowly. If a rovling appeared, she would stop and see what the machine made of the mysterious out of place module. Row by row, she edged the module toward the rails. When she got to the end of the stacks, she took a peek around to check the rails. Six rovlings marched out, pushing and pulling a container. They loaded the railcar as she watched. As they embarked, a fresh railcar came up at the far side.

Telisa returned to the container and brought out the second module. She repeated the long push, moving faster this time. When the coast was clear, Telisa slid the modules over to the rail by the closest door.

Good. Now, how to—

The rail car across the way lifted its metal wheels off the rail and floated over toward her. Telisa cleared out of the way. The car settled back on the rail next to her module.

Nice.

Telisa loaded the modules onto the car. The gate before her opened. Telisa pushed.

Once into the slanting tunnel, Telisa had to work to keep the car slowed. At first her Veer suit's heels slid over the ridges. She grunted and turned her right hip toward the walkway, grabbed the railcar with both arms, and placed the sides of her feet against the railway. Though her feet still slipped over some of the ridges, having the long sides of two feet in contact with the walkway allowed her to slow the descent. Sometimes her feet caught on two different ridges and she halted altogether.

The descent took a long time. Telisa started to let the load go faster for fear of running into rovlings. Finally the side dock came into sight. It occurred to Telisa that she did not know how to direct the load to the side. When the car arrived at the dock, she stopped it cold by placing her feet against a perpendicular surface of the dock. Then she slid the modules off the cart one by one, using brute force.

So much for more brains, less brawn. Sorry, Magnus, maybe next time.

When the cart was empty she released it.

The car moved on down noisily. At first it gained speed, but eventually it seemed to regulate its own descent speed.

By the Five, if I had known it would do that, I could probably have made it here twice as fast.

Telisa stepped forward to figure out the sleds, but they had already come to life. All three of the platforms rose, simultaneously increasing the space between them. Telisa hurriedly dodged aside as they then slid forward and spread out to accept the containers she had brought.

This mission is turning out to be a piece of cake. Hacking the ship will probably be the hardest part.

Telisa loaded the modules on the sleds, then waited to see where they were going to take the cargo, but nothing happened.

Maybe the rovlings guide these things the same way. Seems weird, I know they have the technology to just send the stupid sleds wherever... though I guess the rovlings would need to be there to unload anyway?

Telisa pulled the lead sled. In response, it moved forward under its own power. She decided to pace them and see if she could guide them to the ship. She led them down the first hallway and through an intersection. Telisa could not believe her luck—the first of the modules were being delivered for her!

Suddenly the Rovan machines turned and slid the modules into the triangular side-space of the corridor. Then they moved away.

What the?

Telisa supposed that some other, legitimate, entity had requested work from the machines.

With a sigh heard by no one, Telisa walked up to the first container. After a quick check for rovlings, she grabbed it by one end and pulled it part way out into the corridor. It was heavy, but manageable for her host body.

Telisa found a grip on a ridge across the top of the container and slowly lifted it. Then she walked forward twenty meters and placed it into the side-alcove of the next section of the hallway.

Okay. I can do this. It's just going to take longer. Marcant will have more time.

She saw from the tactical that she was about two-thirds of the way to the ship.

Rovlings appeared down the corridor to the loading dock. Telisa stood up and moved away from the biomodules. Telisa watched as she created more distance. First she counted four, but more rovlings emerged from pipes nearby until eight rovlings were visible.

The rovlings crawled over the biosupply modules. Telisa felt a wave of frustration. She abandoned her crates. As much as she wanted to get them to the Rovan ship, there was no way she could manage it now, short of destroying the rovlings and causing an even greater stir. She gave up her prize.

Telisa strode down the corridor, considering her options. She decided to check in on Marcant.

Telisa saw movement behind her in the video feed from one of her attendants. She slowed. A group of rovlings moved about in the corridor. They walked into the alcoves and others went into rovling pipes. Some even crawled on the ceiling.

For the first time, Telisa doubted her assumption that the rovlings had been tracking the stolen biosupply modules.

They're following me.

Telisa sent her abort signal and chose a different direction at the next intersection. She wanted to give Marcant a good chance of making it back to the rails without being intercepted.

Once around the corner, Telisa shot off at top speed. Her cloaking sphere absorbed all the sound of her passage, though she wondered if it drew more power when she moved quickly. Lee had mentioned that he more challenging the conditions for stealth, the more energy the sphere would need.

She found herself in a new section of the complex. She slowed a little to ponder her choices at the next intersection.

She flipped her tactical to a full three-dimensional display in her mind, showing the parts of the complex they had discovered in the previous trip. She was far above the ship construction center and the level with the force field cells.

For the first time, she wondered if those cells continued on and held more of the alien creatures.

I'm not going to find out.

Telisa headed right, wondering if the level she was on connected with the escape shaft for the newly constructed vessels from the shipyard. The corridor she chose was double-width. The walls to either side extended out as they descended to make the usual triangular side spaces.

I may as well go far from the ship, to give Marcant the best chance of escape. My link can always direct me back.

She ran up to a set of huge doors, one on each side of the hall.

Rovan-sized.

Telisa experienced a moment of hope. Could there be Rovans living here?

The tap of tiny feet distracted Telisa. She checked the direction she had been headed and saw five rovlings advancing toward her. She glanced back. Four more rovlings marched in from that direction. She noticed one hanging back. It had a different kind of device mounted on its top rails than the others.

A sensor rovling. To track me.

Telisa turned back toward the group of five. She noticed one of those rovlings had the same unusual assembly.

Telisa moved. She took three steps forward, planning to charge, but some instinct drew her aside. Two rovling tubes joined the corridor on her right. She knelt and peered inside one. The tube was only about five meters long and emptied into another corridor at the end. Telisa put her arms forward and lunged into the tube with all her strength. She slid through the tube in a long second. She felt no discomfort through her heavy Veer suit.

Telisa emerged into a normal-sized corridor and faced toward the shipyard exit shaft. She ran down the long tunnel until the corridor changed. She saw a familiar counter with a massive rotating doorway of bright red material. A black disk lay overhead.

One of those strange doors. I don't want to get on the wrong side of that.

Telisa did a sharp about-face. As she hurried back, rovlings appeared in a T-intersection ahead.

Telisa flipped on her Rovan force pack and charged. As she reached the rovlings, they reacted.

Pop. Zing. Crack.

Telisa vaulted over three rovlings and landed in against the far wall of the T intersection. She saw another rovling directly ahead, pointing something at her. She judged it was one of the sensors, not a weapon, so she flicked it as she ran past the rovling. The device mounted on it snapped.

Now you see me, now you don't.

Telisa kept running. This time, she consulted her link map for the way back. She turned her force field off to save its energy.

I don't want to start a shitstorm. They seemed kind of laid back while hunting me. Maybe I shouldn't have done that.

The corridor emptied into a room ahead. Telisa charged in. It was a wide-open circular space with no other floor-level exits. Telisa looked upward. It was a small ship berth like the one that held the ship she had discovered with Marcant. She stared at the high walls, looking for a way up. An opening joined the shaft part of the way up.

Telisa received a ping from an attendant hiding in the cargo bay where they had found the biosupply modules. It was one of Marcant's. She believed he was telling her that he had made it back to the shuttle and waited to extract her from the area.

Though pleased with Marcant's timing, Telisa shook her head and clenched her fist.

If only we had the modules. All this for nothing?

Telisa leaped toward the lip of the opening with a single exertion of her powerful legs. She caught the edge in her hands, then performed a smooth muscle-up to gain a perch at the top.

The opening before her was dark. Perhaps a maintenance tunnel? Telisa turned and looked above her. She saw another opening above and sixty degrees to one side, and another.

She repeated her previous maneuver. One glance down showed her that she was gaining dangerous height.

Pop. Pop-Zing. Thwack.

A group of rovlings were shooting at her from below. Telisa leaped again. As she landed on another ledge, her suit flashed an overheat warning. Telisa activated her force pack and leaped again.

I guess the force field wouldn't help much if I fell... or would it? Is it smart enough to absorb impacts with a slow give?

It did not matter. Telisa leaped one more time and reached the top of the shaft. She stood in a huge, round tunnel. The way was almost horizontal, but to her left it angled upward slightly.

She ran that direction. The upward angle steadily increased, but before it became too steep for her to travel, it opened to greet the blue sky above.

"Marcant, are you there? I'm outside now."

"Ah good. I have your location. Pick up?"

"Yes."

Telisa walked out over the rough ground over the newly repaired Rovan shipyard. Her cloaking orb reported an energy crisis, but she was almost out of harm's way.

Telisa's link overlayed the green silhouette of the cloaked shuttle over her vision so she could see Marcant approaching. The Vovokan craft descended rapidly upon her position.

Telisa charged the shuttle and slipped into the open door before it had even settled on the ground. The craft silently powered away. Telisa allowed her exhausted stealth cover to drop.

As soon as the shuttle door closed, Telisa slipped her pack off and dug into it to grab a food packet. She collapsed into her seat and ripped open the packet. She began to assault its contents greedily to satisfy her enhanced body's energy needs.

"Do you at least get control of that ship before leaving?" Telisa demanded through a mouthful of food.

"No. It's too sophisticated," Marcant said.

Telisa growled, startling Marcant. Then she deflated in her chair. "What a waste. We failed," she lamented. "The only other idea I have is to go in shooting with the *Sharplight* and try to capture one of those ships so you can work on it long enough to work out everything we need to know."

"We may not have to do that," Marcant said.

"Do tell," Telisa said.

"While they searched for you back there, I got a lot of communications data. Maybe enough for a breakthrough."

"We came all this way and now you come up with an excuse to chicken out?"

"No, seriously, given the *Sharplight*'s computational resources, I might now be able to crack their communications. Wouldn't you like to talk to them? Or it?"

Telisa sighed.

"Okay. Back to *Sharplight*."

199

Michael McCloskey

Chapter 18

"What's up?" Arakaki asked. Magnus and Yat stood with her in a jagged, dark space within another of the alien ships they had stopped to explore.

"We lost an attendant. Another saw movement near the wreckage," Magnus said.

"Something survived this?" Yat asked.

"No," Arakaki said. "Nothing from *this* ship. But that Rovan battleship out there..."

"Rovlings," Yat concluded.

"Get out of there on the double!" Adair transmitted. "Rovlings are surrounding you!"

They turned and pushed off the way they had come.

"You make a lousy lookout!" Magnus yelled.

"Their approach was obscured by all the wreckage, and they're small," Adair explained.

"Stealth," Magnus ordered. The team winked out of sight. Their ghosts floated in the dark alien wreck. They moved slowly through the bizarre interior.

"Adair! Blast us a way out of here!" Magnus demanded.

"I can't! Two Rovan ships have engaged me! I'm maneuvering away."

"You're going to leave us here?" Arakaki demanded. *Is Adair a traitor like Achaius was?*

"I may be dead before you are," Adair said. The connection dropped.

"That tin ball had *better* be dead," Magnus growled.

"Focus. How are we getting out of this?" Arakaki said.

"We hide," Yat said. "We can't beat them."

"But with our shields, we might escape," Magnus said.

"To...?" Yat asked.

"These spaces are so twisty and dark. We could go back into one of the narrow spirals and squeeze ourselves in," Arakaki said.

"If we had something to put in the way and block them, it might work for a while," Magnus said. "But the rovlings will poke into every hole. One of them will run into us and realize we're here."

"If we can't hide, shouldn't we be getting out of here?" Yat asked. "You said they would run into us in here, even if we're invisible... but outside, there's so much space..."

"Out in open space, they'll all be able to shoot at us," Magnus said. "In here, we only have two approaches to cover."

A rovling appeared from a triangular hole on the ceiling. Arakaki targeted it with her laser. The rovling glowed and melted in the silence of space.

"Make that three," Arakaki said. "There's a hole above us."

"They'll only shoot us if those detector rovlings are out there," Yat said.

"He's got a point," Arakaki said. "We go out and jump in three different directions. They might lose us right away."

Until we run out of energy to stealth ourselves or oxygen to breathe.

Magnus only took a second to decide.

"Okay. On me. This direction," Magnus said.

Arakaki pushed Yat after him and covered their flank. Once they were out of the way, she pushed off after them and let her attendants stabilize her course as she flew backward after them. The dark, jagged inside of the vessel provided a hundred places for rovlings to hide.

Arakaki set her mouth in determination and waited for movement. Sure enough, a rovling darted out from one of the many narrow openings.

Arakaki felt an impact at her hip. Her PAW returned fire. She felt a snap through her suit as it launched a projectile into the vacuum. The rovling fragmented and spiralled back into the darkness.

Arakaki's suit reported itself fully intact. She checked her hip. The laser pistol there had been destroyed by a projectile.

"Dammit!" She detached the weapon and threw it. It spun away into the dead hulk.

"You hit?" Yat asked.

"Little bastard borked my laser pistol," she said.

A slight increase in the ambient lighting told her they had reached the hole they had entered from.

"Here's where we split," Magnus announced.

"What's the plan for rendezvous?" Arakaki asked, though she knew their chances were grim.

"Over there. Meet up at this one," Magnus said. He highlighted one of the many hulks they had noted earlier.

Magnus launched himself sharply to their right and accelerated away from the alien ship.

Arakaki traded looks with Yat's green silhouette.

"Catch you on the other side," she said, and activated her suit jets. She launched herself straight forward.

She watched Yat jump off behind her from an attendant feed.

Arakaki's attendants dropped lower from her perspective until they hovered around her feet, protecting her from fire coming from the ship she had left behind. She ordered them to group closer, then snapped on her force shield.

Moments dragged into minutes as she flew away from the shell of a ship they had been in. The empty void all around her threatened to gnaw a panic into her soul, but Arakaki smashed it down with angry thoughts.

Why do we always end up in the middle of the shooting? The stupid Rovan machines think we're a threat? Why? It must be because the Rovans themselves were aggressors. And Marcant and Maxsym want to grow more of them.

Arakaki floated for ten minutes, putting more distance between herself and the enemy. Finally, she decided to alter her course to nudge her toward the rendezvous point. Rather than use her suit jets, she had the attendants push her. Even with her stealth orb active, the suit jets would eject large particles into space that might give her away; she recalled that Marcant had mentioned that the energy emitted by the attendants was 'much less likely to interact with normal matter', whatever that meant.

She deactivated her force screen. Over the next five minutes her course changed. She traveled a long arc toward the rendezvous ship. On the approach she sized it up. The alien wreck was large. Only two other wrecks of similar size floated nearby.

The skin of the dead hulk was dark gray. Arakaki boosted her visual gain to catch some details. Spiral engravings on the wreck's outer surface glinted for a second in the meager starlight. A hole was visible in the alien vessel, probably its death wound. Suddenly Arakaki felt overwhelmed by the mystery of this dead silent place in the void between the stars.

Where was this ship made? By who? How long ago? Why did they fight?

She looked over toward the dim point of light that was the Rovan battleship.

Do you like being surrounded by the broken ships of your enemies? Is it like leaving skulls out to strike fear into strangers?

Her destination started to grow rapidly. She braked, searching for a good place on the hull to make contact. Arakaki saw a green flicker to her right. She adjusted her course, continuing to slow. The green light resolved into two Terran shapes: she was the last to arrive.

Once she settled in beside them, Yat sent a weak message.

"We have to turn our stealth off," he said. "We can't keep burning energy indefinitely."

"Okay, but we have to get into this fragged ship first," she answered.

Magnus nodded. He pointed toward the hull breach she had noticed on her approach.

Arakaki stepped above the opening and let her attendants cancel her momentum and drive her straight into the alien ship.

"I'm leaving an attendant on watch here," Magnus said. She saw that Magnus had only one attendant left. She had three and Yat had two. Arakaki shook her head.

"No. I have three."

She told an attendant to station at the entrance and watch for rovlings.

Magnus accepted her generosity without comment.

Arakaki knew they were in big trouble. They would run out of air or power soon. It seemed unlikely Adair was still alive and could save them. It also seemed impossible that Telisa and her group would show up soon. For the moment, the three of them had to focus on one problem at a time.

The cross-section of the hole in the ship descended through a bizarre series of gaps in the ship, each less than a meter wide, curved, with smooth inner surfaces.

"It's like a smooth slice cut through a crazy alien fruit," Yat said.

After about five meters, the inside of the ship opened up. Arakaki saw the familiar jagged fractal design of the interior space. Corridors, if that is what they were, opened every few meters. They were crescent-shaped holes that curved off to the unknown. The interior, though complex, was uncluttered. Whenever Arakaki spotted something that might be a piece of equipment, it turned out to be a fragment broken off of the inside in the battle.

Magnus deactivated his stealth. Arakaki and Yat did the same.

"I wonder what Telisa would make of this," Arakaki said. "The aliens were small if they used all these side branches."

"Yes. But I'm still thinking these are robotic ships," Magnus said. "Wouldn't there be tools or beds or… anything scattered around in here if aliens rode inside these spaces?"

"Suppose it was robotic," Yat said. "Wouldn't we see some internal repair machines? The *Sharplight* is full of them."

"Maybe the Rovans sent rovlings in here and killed them all, or dragged them all away as prisoners!" Arakaki said.

"That would be a good thing," Yat said. "If they take prisoners, we might survive. As it is, we're running out of air. We need a plan."

"Yes. I'm thinking," Magnus said. "The only idea I have right now is to send out an open distress signal. If Adair doesn't come get us, the Rovans will."

"I can improve upon that slightly," Arakaki said. "Send out an attendant broadcasting a signal as a distraction. Have the signal communicate our real position. The Rovans shouldn't be able to understand it."

"My attendants are picking up a power source ahead," Yat said. "Maybe we could siphon off some energy and get some more time for stealth and force fields."

So that we can suffocate in safety, Arakaki thought.

They continued down the main hollow in the spine of the vessel. The walls looked like the jagged ribs of a giant with spaces in between that led off to smaller and smaller side tunnels.

Suddenly Arakaki's suit reported overheating.

Arakaki's training took over. Her had her attendants press her to the deck, then she pushed off with her left arm and rolled to her right toward a jagged wall.

"What the—" Yat started.

"Laser!" Arakaki barked.

Yat and Magnus broke to either side, searching for cover. They slipped partially into two different crescent-shaped niches in the other wall.

"So much for walking in and stealing some energy," Yat said.

"Did anyone see the source?" Arakaki asked. The heating had stopped, but she was uncomfortable. The suit could not radiate or sink all of the energy fast enough. She groaned in her suit but did not broadcast it.

"Not at all," Magnus said. "I can't understand anything about this place."

"Okay, so we turn on our force screens and hit the source when it hits us," Arakaki summarized. As soon as she said it, her attendant notified her of the approach of rovlings.

"Something on our six, right?" Yat asked.

"Yes. They're coming. Now we're trapped," Arakaki said grimly. "We have to disable that laser or we'll die here." She did not mention that they were probably going to die here one way or another regardless.

She held her PAW vertically and straightened against the wall, readying herself to move.

"No, wait. Don't disable it!" Magnus said. "These things are enemies, remember? These aliens and the Rovans."

"So what? We're stuck between them," Yat said.

"We have a little bit of stealth time left. We go invisible, cross this area and each go to one of those three crescents in the corridor beyond."

"Are you sure those corridors aren't in the fire arc of the laser?" Yat asked.

"I'm not one hundred percent, but it doesn't look like it from here," Magnus answered.

"Seems like we'll be trapped there, too," Yat said.

"At least that puts the laser between us and the rovlings," Arakaki said.

Yat nodded. "Okay, it's a good idea."

Arakaki turned on her stealth sphere. A moment later she was running across the wavy alien floor. An array of dark narrow openings flashed by. Then she found a major niche and turned sharply into it.

Yat came in after her. Magnus chose an opening on the other side, directly across from them. Arakaki checked the ceiling. It did have a spike or two that might have been a laser emitter, but she could not tell.

Magnus turned his stealth off. Her attendant told her that he had activated his force screen.

"Nothing," he said. "We're out of sight of the weapon, whatever it was."

Yat and Arakaki went visible.

Arakaki watched the feed from an attendant retreating from the rovlings. Soon it would have no place to go. It was smart enough to see the threat of the laser on the tactical. She did not know which enemy the device would have a better chance of avoiding, but she did not want to drain the laser's power. She told the attendant to try to pass the rovlings on full evasive.

The attendant zipped toward the rovlings. It fell off the tactical.

"That was our last set of eyes—" Yat started.

Vibrations came through the hull.

Thump. Snap.

A piece of debris flew past.

They're fighting!

"Okay, this is great, but we need to give them the slip again," Yat pointed out.

"This way," Magnus said. "My tunnel curves up and away toward the… aft, I think?"

209

"Okay. I'll send one attendant down this side just in case we need an alternate route," Arakaki said.

"Yat, turn on your screen and come across," Magnus said.

Yat ran the gap and made it to Magnus's side. Then they fled down the tunnel. Arakaki followed a few seconds later.

The slender corridor closed in. It became even more cramped inside. Magnus and Yat were already slipping through sideways. Soon Arakaki had to do the same.

The entire corridor tilted ahead. The right wall slowly became the new 'floor'. Magnus started to crawl. He turned on one of his lights to see ahead.

Vibrations came through the hull.

They're still fighting back there.

The space continued to narrow. Magnus slowed.

"This is the end of the line? We're stuck," Yat said.

"We have to find another way out," Arakaki said. "Maybe we head back—"

Suddenly, a sound came through the walls she pressed against.

Ruuuuummmmble.

The interior of the ship bucked into Arakaki brutally. She started to spin. Energetic vibrations could be heard through her suit where it contacted the ship and from vaporized molecules hitting her on their hurried way out into the void. The sound rapidly faded back into the placid silence of space broken only by her rapid heartbeat.

The ship has shattered!

Her attendants stabilized her relative to a piece of the ship. She was no longer confined to a tight space; most of her perimeter was now wide open. She checked her status. Her suit told her she did not have any broken bones.

"Yat?"

"I'm... here..."

"Magnus?"

There was no response. A red pane in Arakaki's PV told her Yat had been injured. A puncture wound in his leg. Arakaki took out her medikit with practiced efficiency. She activated it and let it confer with Yat's Veer suit.

"It's asking me to align it with your leg," Arakaki said. She checked her tactical again. There were still no signs of the rovlings, but she had no faith that would remain the case for longer than a minute or two.

This is bad. The kit wouldn't ask me to do this if it didn't have to cut into him.

Yat did not answer. The medikit overlayed its desired position over her version. Arakaki aligned it as instructed. The medikit got a connection with Yat's Veer suit and negotiated a cut through its defenses. The device formed an airtight seal with Yat's leg and opened a slit to the flesh beyond.

Arakaki saw a bit of blood spatter inside the seal.

"Are you still with me?" she asked. Yat's suit reported him to be alive. His heart rate was slowing, but that could be a good thing.

"I'm good," Yat asserted quickly. "The medikit repaired the artery that was bleeding when it pulled out the fragment, and now my suit has given me several chemical gifts. Believe me, I'm feeling no pain."

"That means little," Arakaki protested.

"The suit says I'm at eighty-five percent."

"Seventy-three percent, you liar," Arakaki said. "You think I'm not monitoring your injury from here?"

Yat shrugged.

"Now we find Magnus," he said. Suddenly his tactical ghost flickered and flashed. He became fully visible.

"Not good," he summarized.

This isn't another practice session. It's real. We're going to die.

Despite the grim thoughts, Arakaki was calm. They had made it through training scenarios that looked worse than this.

Arakaki turned her stealth off.

"What are you doing!? Yours still has energy," Yat said. His anger only half managed to wash the pain out of his voice.

"I'm not going to survive another…" she snapped, then could not finish.

I won't outlive someone so close again.

"Turn your stealth back on and go find him," Yat said. "I'll wait here for you to get back."

"We have our shields. We'll kill whatever comes," she stated stubbornly. "Let's go. Magnus can't be far, he was right above us."

"Maybe his attendants kept him close to the other piece of the ship," Yat suggested. "Find that piece, and we find him."

Ping. Snap. Thwack.

Rovling projectiles started to rain in around them. Arakaki could not hear the sounds of the shooting, but the dull impact vibrations of the projectiles were audible within her suit.

Arakaki put up her shield and turned toward her attackers. Her weapon targeted and fired at several of them.

Rattle. Rattle.

The muted vibrations of her weapon came through her hands. More rovlings appeared along a curved edge of the alien ruin beside them.

Rattle. Rattle. Rattle.

One of Arakaki's attendants darted left then right before her, then struck the side of the alien ship. It spiralled away in silence.

Arakaki's tactical showed her that Yat was engaged as desperately as she was. A Rovan ship appeared in the distance. It was bigger than a shuttle but smaller than a Terran destroyer.

Ping. Thwack.
Rattle. Rattle. Rattle.

Arakaki lost her last attendant. She took a look left and right. Rovlings were literally everywhere. She told her breaker claw to hit the alien ship, but the device told her the target was too far away.

Rattle. Rattle. Rattle.

"I can't hold them!" Yat transmitted urgently.

And this time there's no one to save us.

A binder helix snapped out from one of the rovlings and passed by Arakaki on her left. She knew what was next. A powerful pull yanked her backward. Her back struck Yat, then she was stuck. Her stun baton was pulled back behind her. The rovlings closed in on her.

I wish I still had that grenade around my neck.

Michael McCloskey

Chapter 19

Marcant checked a new pane asking for attention in his PV. A new analysis result had come through on one of the scores of Rovan communications experiments he had running. Marcant sat up in his VR lounge on the *Sharplight*.

"I've made a breakthrough," Marcant announced on the PIT channel.

"Can you talk to the Rovans?" Telisa asked, ever to the point.

"Talk, no. But limited communication, maybe. I've been experimenting with the data from the incident with that alien that attached itself to our hull. Turns out that when they sent us that location pointer in our formats, they also tried to tell us their own location pointer formats and frequencies. And more recently, when those rovlings were searching for you, they were reporting your suspected location back and forth. So I figured out how to send them a location pointer."

"Is that going to be enough to make real progress?" Barrai asked.

"My initial thinking is along these lines... first, I'll send them our location. Then I'll send them their location. That should demonstrate to them that we understand how to express coordinates using their methods. Then we send them the location of the three stations."

"Interesting," Telisa said.

"Clever," Maxsym admitted.

He could have said 'genius'.

"But what response do you expect?" Telisa asked.

"We have some empty biosupply modules from S3," Maxsym said. "Suppose we send some to them. That, together with the location of the nursery stations should be enough for them to understand."

"Maybe…" Telisa said slowly. Her voice sounded hopeful, positive.

"It could also draw them out here to attack us again," Barrai said.

"I think they know we're out here. The fleet just doesn't want to abandon the planet," Telisa said.

"If we can communicate with them at all, even only locations, that can only help our situation," Maxsym said. "Right now we're a mysterious enemy to them. The idea that we're willing to talk could change their whole picture of us."

Marcant knew their leader felt profound disappointment at the way so many of their Rovan interactions had ended with fighting. Each time Telisa had wanted to remain peaceful, to learn to communicate and get to know the Rovans, and several times she had failed. It was not because of overt Rovan aggression; each time the Rovans must have felt they were making reasonable responses.

Marcant kept in mind that there had been at least one time they had worked together. The Rovans or their AI had sent out a ship to help when they disassembled the dangerous alien creature.

"It depends on what they're like," Marcant said. "But the rovlings didn't attack us on sight. So they're not bloodthirsty."

It was an easy sell. Telisa wanted to be allies with the Rovans. There was no way she would turn down a real attempt at communication.

"Start the process," Telisa said. "Send them the two local locations for a while to make sure they're getting it. Barrai, pack up a few modules so that a shuttle can send them off."

Marcant started the transmissions. He noticed that some of the *Sharplight*'s local communications arrays had been destroyed and remained unreplaced. Marcant had only himself to blame—he had avoided repair work at every turn. He knew it was vital, but nothing agonized him more than the drudgery of simple work.

He told the *Sharplight* to send the message twice a minute. After two minutes, he received a reply. It was an echo of his transmission, but with the two locations reversed.

"They got it," he said.

"They noticed it fast," Telisa said.

"*It* noticed the message quickly," Marcant said. *It's an AI for sure.*

"Maybe," she said.

"Okay I'm sending them the locations of the three stations," Marcant announced.

Everyone stopped talking on the channel. Marcant watched the messages go out from a standard Space Force communications panel in his PV.

After a few minutes, Marcant decided there would not be a response. Telisa was not ready to give up, though.

"Send them the modules," Telisa ordered.

"Aye, TM," Barrai responded.

Soon the bay doors opened to let a shuttle out. Several empty biosupply modules were attached at its nose. The payload accelerated toward the Rovan squadron.

Marcant fidgeted while the modules gained speed. He had a sudden urge for a glucosoda. He grabbed one from his local cache and started sipping away.

"That's good enough. Bring our shuttle back," Telisa ordered.

Marcant still sat on the edge of his seat. He could not find much attention for anything else than watching the course of the payload and the Rovan ships. The minutes passed in agony.

"One Rovan ship is matching course with our present," Barrai said. Her voice remained level.

"They'll have it soon!" Marcant said.

"Excellent. This might work," Telisa said.

"What now?" Maxsym asked.

Marcant felt excited and impatient. Would they finally be able to stop skirmishing with Rovans?

"Now we wait," Telisa said.

Marcant sighed.

***

A high priority message woke Marcant. Several objects had been launched toward their position in the outer system.

By Zappelhammers it worked!

Barrai and Telisa were already chatting about the news.

"The objects are headed right toward us," Barrai said. "Definitely not Rovan vessels, at least not like any we've seen."

"Biosupply modules?" Telisa asked, hoping out loud.

"We'll know soon," Barrai said. "I advise caution."

"Amazing! Let's intercept and load them," Maxsym said.

"No!" Marcant said.

"What? We've communicated with the Rovans, and it looks like they responded in the best possible way," Telisa said.

"Maybe it's a trap," he said.

"This is the race you want to resurrect?" Barrai asked.

"I tell you what, if they try to blow us up, I'll seriously reconsider my position on making more Rovans," Marcant said.

"Hold here. Send out five attendants to meet these packages before they get too close. I want it checked out," Telisa said. She sounded as excited as Marcant felt.

The attendants met with the cargo over a light second out. All their scans quickly verified the best case scenario: complete biosupply modules.

Please let it not be a trap.

"Can we safely stow these materials in our holds?"

"The attendants have scanned every module. There is no apparent danger," Barrai said.

Telisa's lips compressed.

"We know the Rovans have technology superior to ours, at least in some areas," she said.

Marcant figured he had planted the seed of doubt in her mind. Now she was being paranoid.

"I have the solution," Marcant said.

"Yes?"

"Where are the Rovans weak? In their security. So, we hack these bio modules and take control of them. That way, if they're bombs, we can prevent their activation. There will be no way for the Rovans to detonate them remotely."

"So you take control of the known electronic systems. There might be a hidden detonation system, isolated from the rest. It might be only a few hundred molecules big," Barrai said.

Marcant shrugged. It was possible.

"All right, we have to take a risk. We'll minimize that risk by looking for traps for another day or two. Brainstorm some possible angles we haven't thought of yet," Telisa said.

"Aye, TM," Barrai said.

Marcant remained in a good mood despite the delay. He finally let go of his impatience. What was another day? They were about to resurrect a civilization.

***

Marcant watched from his VR chair as the *Sharplight* brought the modules aboard. His quarters were dark, just the way he liked it. All the interesting input came to his brain from outside the room.

"The last of the modules are aboard," Barrai reported.

"And no boom," Marcant noted from his perch.

"Good. Now we can go resupply the stations and watch them make more Rovans," Telisa said.

"What? We're going ahead with it right now?" Barrai asked.

"They gave us the supplies. That means they understand exactly what we mean to do, and approve," Telisa said. "That tips the scales in my mind."

"We never actually saw any Rovans..." Barrai protested.

She doesn't see this as Rovan buy-in, Marcant thought.

"If my race was mostly extinct, maybe I'd be shy as well," Maxsym said.

"It's a Rovan AI left that runs that military installation. I think it's mission is to protect the colony," Marcant said. "That's why the ships don't go there themselves to resupply the stations. It's too far off-mission. They must have created the AI with some fairly strong intrinsic motivation limitations."

"Interesting theory," Barrai said.

"Do you have another?" Marcant challenged.

"No, but is the go-ahead from such an AI any good? The point is, this is still guesswork."

"I'll think on it, and when we meet back up with the rest of the team, we'll discuss it again," Telisa said.

She's going to do it. I know she will.

Michael McCloskey

Chapter 20

Magnus crawled out of a crevice in the alien hulk. The room spun. He shook his head to clear it, but he still felt wobbly. He stopped to recover. After a minute, he noticed a pattern to the sensation.

Oh. It's not me. This thing really is spinning.

The explosion must have given his piece of the hulk significant angular momentum.

One attendant stood at station with a meter of him. It was not Legbreaker. The attendant had a prominent scratch across its surface but reported itself to be at one hundred percent.

He checked his air. He had less than an hour left.

Magnus needed to know if there were any rovlings in the fragment with him. He told the attendant to check the hulk. He watched it explore through his PV.

It looked as though he was alone on the ship fragment. Magnus carefully moved toward the axis of rotation. The effects of the spin lessened.

If Adair is gone, then there's no hope.

Magnus looked around. He saw a circular seal on the chaotic wall. He told the attendant to return and scan it. Was there air on the other side?

For some reason he stared at the seal again. Even in his dire situation, he could not suppress his curiosity. What was it?

Magnus reached out and touched the wall. The surface was smooth. He looked around the room again. It looked just like the rest of these alien hulks: dark, jagged, and rife with mysterious narrow gaps too small to investigate directly. Yet the seal before him was smooth and perfectly round.

This is the only round thing I've seen in one of these ships.

Suddenly an urge to vomit struck him. He reeled, retching for a long moment. Then his suit injected something that calmed his system.

He withdrew his hand. As he pulled his fingers away, something rotated slightly.

What the—?

He put his hand on the circle again and twisted. The dial moved with his hand, counterclockwise. He managed to turn it perhaps one radian before it stopped. The perimeter lit up with white light.

Way to go, idiot. You probably activated the self-destruct.

Despite the thought, Magnus was not afraid. His situation was grim, so why not experiment?

The circle rose from its emplacement and floated away. He could now see it was a disc only about two centimeters thick. Behind the apparent lid, a recession held a cylinder just the right size for his hand. One end expanded into a wider cone, the other end sharpened into a point.

The prize is mine. Whatever the hell it is.

Magnus grabbed the object and put it into his pack. Then he wondered why he had even bothered when he was about to die anyway.

This is why Telisa is such a good partner for me. For all my cynicism, she's the positive antidote.

Magnus pondered how to spend his remaining time.

If I stay hidden here, I die with a probability of one. Oh, wait. I'm assuming Adair is dead. If the AI managed to live and is searching for me now, there might be hope. Call it ninety-seven percent chance of death.

Magnus decided to have his attendant send out a ping. Maybe it could call more attendants that could haul him somewhere, or maybe Adair was still alive.

At first, Magnus thought to send a location ping with an SOS message. Then he realized that if Yat and Arakaki got that message, they might risk their lives to come here for nothing.

I need to make sure they're focused on their own survival.

He set up the SOS packet to send their links a message: "Just calling for extraction by Adair or attendants. Don't risk yourselves to come here, there's no air here. Save yourselves!".

Magnus contemplated it.

They will ignore that. I could make it an order, but they still might ignore it.

He changed the message to: "I'm dead. Save yourselves!".

Not good enough.

Magnus had worked with the Veer suits his whole life. In that time, he had picked up a few tricks. The Veer suit could communicate with links. He had a series of one-time codes that would work with any of the Veer suits the team had in inventory. He could add codes to have the Veer suits send a bogus death notification to the wearer. They would think he had died immediately after sending the SOS.

If they dig into it, they'll see the deception. But they won't. They'll believe it without question.

Magnus hesitated.

If Adair saves them first, they'll tell Adair I'm dead. Then I will have gutted my slight chance of survival.

He shook his head. Why the indecision?

My oxygen is dropping.

Magnus left his SOS message in place and sent it without the bogus death notification.

He drifted in the hulk, waiting for any result. The attendant peeked out here and there, keeping Magnus aware of the area.

Magnus thought of his time with Telisa as he watched his supply readouts drop.

Minutes later, a sharp vibration came through the structure.

Someone came!

Magnus reactivated his stealth orb and sent his last attendant out through the open side of the hull to investigate.

It was not Adair or an attendant. Mechanical octopeds crawled about outside, looking for a way in. Magnus switched from his stealth device to his force screen, which had more energy left anyway.

If I do nothing, I die. I have to fight, right?

Magnus struggled to concentrate.

If I let them take me, there's a chance. If the Rovans were good guys I might live.

Magnus hesitated. Was his choice between certain death vs a chance at life or death... or between death vs a chance at life or something *worse* than death? Would the rovlings rip him limb from limb? Or would they capture him? Would he be a tortured prisoner of the Rovans?

Their technology is advanced. They wouldn't need me for experiments.

With a few scans and some samples, they would know everything about him. Simulations would reveal all the rest to them; all Terran physical strengths and weaknesses.

But it would take Trilisk level tech to decode my consciousness and learn everything I know.

Could the Rovans potentially torture him to gain his knowledge? Maybe they would pull out his link, learn how it worked, and forcibly install their own link that could put him into VR without his knowledge or control. Then they could torment him with deceptive games for years to learn what he knew, how he thought, how he behaved.

"Magnus, you are one cynical bastard," he said aloud.

He tossed away his weapons one by one.

Let's give it a go and see what they do with me.

Michael McCloskey

Chapter 21

Telisa walked into the lounge for an incarnate meeting. Only half of the team was present, as Magnus, Arakaki, and Yat had not yet returned. The *Sharplight* sat on station near the Rovan stations in the Guiholda Conchallon system.

"We've waited long enough," Telisa said. "It's time to get those biosupply modules over there."

"It'll be tricky," Maxsym said. "The rovlings won't let us just walk in there."

"Marcant and I can handle it," Telisa said.

"What? Me again?"

"This should be old hat for you by now, Marcant," Telisa said.

"We've only done a couple of incursions among hostile rovlings!"

"For someone as smart as you are, that's old hat," Telisa said.

"Flattery doesn't work on me, you have to have a logical argument," Marcant said.

Telisa's brows knitted and she opened her mouth to fire back, but she hesitated to order him to do it.

I should tell him it's the only way that—

"Okay, never mind, I'll do it," Marcant said. He must have anticipated her response and cut to the chase. He had been chafing to do this since the idea first came up.

Telisa nodded. "Good. Barrai, prepare another distraction battalion," Telisa said.

"It was a close thing last time," Marcant pointed out.

"Double the size of the distraction force," Telisa ordered.

"Aye, TM."

Telisa knew Barrai was not too happy about the decision to supply the Rovan station, even though they had received supplies from Rovans or a Rovan AI. Adair and Marcant believed it was a Rovan AI that was either very limited in scope of intellect, or perhaps that it had been traumatized by the loss of its Rovan creators. Did it refuse to leave the colony out of fear, or a sense of duty, or because it simply had no free will?

"This will be a breeze," Telisa said. "We don't need to sneak in at all. If we can find some cargo bay doors, hack them open, and drop these modules off, I'm sure the rovlings can take care of the rest."

"You're probably right," Maxsym said. "A Rovan supply ship would drop these modules off and the station must know how to distribute the contents into all the various vats and containers."

Telisa reviewed the maps of S1. She remembered a lot about the station, including that it had large outer doors opening into apparent cargo bays, but she had not remembered the exact locations.

"How about here?" Telisa said. She sent a pointer referring them to a set of doors big enough to accept the biosupply modules. "The attendant mapping S1 discovered a series of tubes leading to many of the central tanks on the station here. It seems a reasonable guess that a biosupply module might be drained from this bay."

"It's a good location to try," Maxsym said.

"Gear up!" Telisa said. She loved saying that. If only Magnus were here with them. She rose to her feet and loped out. She gathered her OCP gear and coordinated with Marcant to arrange for their shuttle. She met Marcant at the bay fifteen minutes later.

"Here we are again," Telisa said.

"Again?"

"Old hat, remember?" Telisa said. "You with us, Maxsym?"

"Yes, I'm monitoring you. Since you're not a simulationist like your teammate, Telisa, I'll just say good luck."

"I might be a simulationist in another reality on the stack," Telisa joked. Marcant actually smiled. She leaped up the ramp. He followed.

"Stay alert and this'll be a float in the chamber," she said out loud.

"You need to connect to SolNet more often," he said. "You speak like a... person your age."

Telisa smiled. She had better things to do than worry about how Core Worlders talked this week.

Barrai had used robotics to move the fifty biosupply modules out of the *Sharplight*. The shuttle rendezvoused with the module package and attached itself.

"This will be trickier than the shuttle alone, but I've made the calculations based on our previous slip-throughs," Barrai informed them. "We can handle it by using an extra energy weapon burst to suppress the Rovan shields for a second longer."

Marcant did not look happy. "Don't forget to tell us when to turn our force packs on," he said nervously.

"Will do. I have your helm," Barrai announced.

The shuttle moved closer to the station with the biomodules in tow. As Telisa waited for everything to line up, she wondered what Magnus was doing.

"Turn your Rovan packs on now. On your command, TM," Barrai said.

Telisa gave Marcant a look. He turned on his shield and nodded.

"Go."

The *Sharplight* lit up Rovan station's shields. The ride was a little rougher than before, but the shuttle slipped through. Telisa's instruments showed her the modules had made it, too.

They maneuvered toward the incursion point. Barrai was still busy getting three more shuttles of robots through. The *Sharplight* fired again. The tactical showed three more shuttles on their side of the shield, but one was red.

Telisa's PV told her communications with the *Sharplight* were delayed by a couple of seconds. Barrai was having some trouble getting through the shield, but having several shuttles and a bunch of attendants helped cut through.

"Some damage... on that one," Barrai said. "The cargo is intact, though... You'll have your distraction in T minus... three minutes."

They exited the shuttle and sized up the biomodules. They had been packed in groups of five. Telisa, Marcant, and ten attendants gave the first group of five biomodules a modest momentum toward the station bay doors.

"Get the doors open for us, Marcant," Telisa ordered. "I'll line up the rest of the modules."

Marcant jetted past the modules and fired up his Rovan hacking suite. Telisa started the modules drifting gently toward the doors. A minute passed with no results.

"Going well," Marcant said. "It's taking longer because these big doors seem to have a few more safety features than the smaller locks."

Telisa nodded in her suit. She had not given the modules their full momentum, just in case. Now she was glad she had been conservative.

The lock doors began to open. Once the span of a meter grew between them, a squad of attendants darted in to scout for danger.

"There's activity inside," Marcant announced.

"Force field packs back on," Telisa ordered. "Let's get this over with."

Marcant nodded in his space suit. The bay doors sped up. Soon a bright white bay with several red stripes could be seen beyond. A series of long, segmented containers were secured to one wall. Rovlings perched on some of them, facing toward the opening bay doors. They fired at the attendants.

Marcant took a few shots with his PAW to suppress the rovlings within. Telisa focused on gently accelerating the first group of modules through.

I wonder how hard of an impact these things can take.

"There's too many of them," Marcant said. "The force field is the only reason I'm not already in trouble."

"Just get... the modules in there," Maxsym urged from the *Sharplight*. His words came in with delays because of the Rovan shielding.

"They're *shooting* at us," Marcant told him.

"That's good... they're not shooting... at the module," Maxsym joked. "Use it as cover!"

"No," Telisa said. "This batch is on the way in. Take station over there and hold them. I'm going to get the next group."

Smack.

Something struck her screen.

"Hold them? Just me?" Marcant complained, but he accelerated out from behind the module that was crossing into the bay and took the position outside the doors where she had indicated.

Telisa sent four attendants zipping out to the other biosupply modules. She decided they may as well get them all moving faster. If they took their time and gently put one batch into the bay at a time, the number of rovlings might grow unmanageable.

She accelerated the second set of modules through.

Ping. Snap.

Telisa looked out across the station. There were rovlings crawling along the outside of the station hull.

"Rovlings coming in behind you, Marcant," Telisa said.

Marcant turned and shot some of the rovlings flanking him. Telisa watched the tactical. All their attendants hid behind the modules, pushing them toward the doors.

"Okay, I'm coming out to help draw some fire," Telisa said. She gave a module pack one last nudge and floated out into view on the opposite side of Marcant's position.

Telisa took a laser in each hand and picked off more rovlings.

"We've got half of them in... Marcant... stop killing them!" Maxsym transmitted.

"What? We're not defending ourselves?"

"Those rovlings... are probably supposed... to take care of the young! We can't kill... too many of them."

"Not only am I supposed to get shot at, I can't shoot back," Marcant grumbled, positioning himself close to the module.

"Keep going!" Maxsym urged.

"Okay, cool it Maxsym, unless you see something dangerous," Telisa ordered. "Marcant, focus on the task at hand, please."

Marcant's constant complaining made her miss Magnus. At least Marcant had learned to obey whilst emitting his stream of complaints.

I suppose I'm asking a lot of my computation specialist. But Siobhan liked this kind of thing and she wasn't a combat specialist.

"I'm changing position to get out of this crossfire," Marcant reported. He blinked out of sight as he activated his stealth sphere.

Telisa took out another two rovlings. She also changed position to buy time.

"This is too many. My force field is weakening. Something got through!"

"Not much longer," Telisa said. The attendants had finally gotten all the modules up to a reasonable velocity relative to the station.

"Look. These things are fairly smart. If we leave the last few out here, the rovlings might collect them," Marcant said.

"Are you sure? Do you want to have to come back through the shields again?" Telisa asked.

"Yes," Marcant transmitted nervously.

Telisa took a second, then made her decision.

"Okay, get back to shuttle right now."

The tactical showed Marcant launch himself toward the shuttle.

Telisa positioned herself and launched after him a few seconds later, but with much more power. If energy beams hit her shield as she left the scene, Telisa could not detect them within the shield. She landed on top of the shuttle and grasped protrusions on the surface with strong fingers. Then she pushed off with her legs on the opposite side and somersaulted into the airlock from above.

They cycled through and clambered into the vehicle. Telisa heard a snapping noise and realized small projectiles were raining onto the skin of the shuttle.

Telisa checked the situation through the shuttle's sensors. Outside, the rovlings swarmed over the last few modules as if searching for remaining enemies. Then, two rovlings leaped out of the bay trailing cables to connect to the cargo.

"See? They're gathering them," Marcant said.

"Good call," Telisa said. Telisa turned her attention toward their extraction from behind the station force screen. The shuttle edged away from the station. Barrai was trying to synchronize the extraction from the other side of the shield.

It's done. I can't wait to see what happens in there.

Chapter 22

Telisa watched the Rovan station S2 from a lounge on the *Sharplight*. Four more days had passed with no appearance from the other half of the team that had left on the *Iridar* to search for living Rovans at another colony site.

I'm getting as fidgety as Marcant just sitting around waiting for Magnus to come back, or this station to do something dramatic.

Telisa had already been doing long workouts, crazy VR training sessions, and revisiting old Trilisk notes to burn her time. Still, she found herself sitting in this lounge for an hour every day, waiting and trying to figure out how to make something happen faster.

She checked the position of their robotic spy. It took a couple of minutes for snippets to come through from the Rovan station. Rovlings moved busily through a large room, carrying unrecognizable tools or containers. No young Rovans had made an appearance.

Clearly this will take time. Ugh.

"We have to go look for the others," Telisa announced on the team channel. She offered a video feed and connected to the others with feeds of their own.

"We can't leave now!" Maxsym protested.

"What?" demanded Marcant.

"This will take time. We have missing team members."

"Maybe we can move to S3 and watch from there," Maxsym said. "You go without us."

"Ridiculous! What if the rovlings came to reclaim the station?" Telisa asked.

"Well, we have stealth spheres and... you could leave a shuttle behind, just in case."

"A shuttle. In a heavily irradiated system with that Rovan patrol ship roaming around? No. Look, I'm as eager to meet the new Rovans as you are. We'll be back. It's going to take time for them to grow and learn anyway."

"It's hard to say. I suspect the process is highly optimized over their natural reproductive methods," Maxsym said.

"The others could be in trouble. We're going next shift. You have three hours. I suggest you arrange for some attendants or probes to stay behind and record the transmissions from our spybot. We don't want to lose any information if they happen to find it while we're gone."

Maxsym nodded in his video feed. Marcant said nothing, which meant he agreed.

"I wonder where that patrol ship is," Telisa said. "I'm of a mind to stop at the mining station and 'borrow' some of the materials stockpiled there. We need supplies for the rest of the repairs... and to make more robots."

"Now that's a great idea," Barrai said.

"You're turning your best two scientists into space pirates?" Marcant asked dryly.

Telisa did not talk about the awful feeling in her gut. Were the others not back because something was wrong? What if she had already waited too long to go looking for them?

THE END of The Rovan Binary (continued in The Rovan Trap)

From the Author

Thanks for reading! As an indie author, I rely on your ratings and reviews to legitimize my work to those who have not read me. Please rate and review this book online.

Made in the USA
Middletown, DE
03 June 2019